Emily Forbes is an award-winning author of Medical Romance for Mills & Boon. She has written over 25 books and has twice been a finalist in the Australian Romantic Book of the Year Award, which she won in 2013 for her novel *Sydney Harbour Hospital: Bella's Wishlist*. You can get in touch with Emily at emilyforbes@internode.on.net, or visit her website at emily-forbesauthor.com.

REUNITED WITH HER BROODING SURGEON

EMILY FORBES

MILLS & BOON

First published in Great Britain 2018
by Mills & Boon, an imprint of HarperCollins*Publishers*
1 London Bridge Street, London, SE1 9GF

Large Print edition 2019

© 2018 Emily Forbes

ISBN: 978-0-263-07812-1

MIX
Paper from
responsible sources
FSC
www.fsc.org   FSC™ C007454

This book is produced from independently certified FSC™ paper to ensure responsible forest management. For more information visit www.harpercollins.co.uk/green.

Printed and bound in Great Britain
by CPI Group (UK) Ltd, Croydon, CR0 4YY

To the fabulous Amy Andrews,

We've done it again!

Thank you—it's always fun
to write with a friend.
Wishing you happy days as we send
Grace, Marcus, Lola and Hamish
out into the world.

CHAPTER ONE

'DID YOU JUST say you have a spare kidney?'

Grace smiled. She knew her phone call would cause Connie Matera some disbelief but she also knew that would rapidly give way to relief and excitement once she explained the situation to her. 'Yes. I have a spare kidney and it's going to be yours,' she repeated.

'Did someone die?'

As the renal transplant co-ordinator at one of Sydney's biggest hospitals Grace knew that for transplant recipients their good fortune was often tinged with guilt that someone had died in order to give them what they needed. But that wasn't the case this time. 'No. It's from a living donor.'

'How—why?' Grace could hear Connie struggling to find the right words, to ask the right questions. 'How do you just get a spare kidney?'

'You've heard of the paired kidney exchange programme?' Grace asked.

'Yes. But I thought I needed to have someone, a family member or friend, who was prepared to give up a kidney in exchange for one for me? I thought that was how it worked.'

'Normally, yes, but you got lucky.' Grace knew that Connie's family had offered to donate a kidney to her but, while her sister and mother had the same blood type, their tissue type hadn't been a match and therefore they hadn't been suitable donors. Which had left Connie having regular dialysis and waiting on the transplant list for a deceased donor. Until now. 'One of our patients on the exchange programme was a match with a deceased donor so now they don't need their living donation. That donor has offered to give their kidney anyway and you are the best match on the transplant list.'

'A stranger is voluntarily giving me their kidney?'

'Yes.'

'Has that ever happened before?'

'Not to my knowledge.' Was it fear or scepticism Grace could hear in Connie's voice? She didn't want her to refuse this offer. It was too generous and meant too much. 'This is good news, Connie. It's your lucky day.'

Grace heard Connie's deep intake of breath. 'Yes, yes. Of course it is. What do we do now?'

'I know you're scheduled for dialysis tomorrow but can you come in today at two for a pre-op appointment? We need to run some tests and I'm hoping to get your surgery scheduled for next week.'

'That soon?'

'Your donor was already scheduled for surgery next Wednesday as part of a paired kidney exchange exercise. The theatres and hospitals are all booked and your donor is happy to go ahead as planned, albeit with a different recipient. If I can get one more theatre here, and if all your pre-op tests are good, we'll add you to the list.'

'No more dialysis?'

'Hopefully this time next week, no more dialysis,' Grace confirmed. 'I'll see you at two.'

'Okay.'

'And, Connie,' Grace added with a smile in

her voice, 'buy a lottery ticket on your way in here.'

She was still smiling as she said goodbye and hung up the phone. She loved this part of her job. As a member of the organ donation team it wasn't often she got to deliver good news without a side serving of sad news. But in the case of the paired kidney exchange programme, where living donors selflessly offered their organs, it was a rewarding part of the job and Grace was excited.

Some days were tough. Delivering bad news to people was never easy but today was a good day. Today she had a kidney to give away. And today she was going to be busy. The phone call to Connie had been the first piece in the final puzzle. All the other donors and recipients were checked and ready to go. Their surgeries were scheduled for next week but she needed to book one more theatre for Connie and pray that her tests results were what they needed to be. Then she needed to keep her fingers crossed that no one got sick between now and then. Or changed their minds.

She had twelve surgeries to schedule across

five different hospitals in three different cities. It was going to be the biggest paired kidney exchange exercise that had ever occurred in Australia and she was part of it. She'd been working in the transplant unit for the past two years but had only recently been promoted to the co-ordinator position. She'd been involved in paired kidney exchange operations before but nothing of this magnitude.

She entered Connie's details into the nephrologist's appointment calendar and made sure all the relevant documents, recent test results, new test request forms and consent forms were attached before making a courtesy call to Connie's GP. Hopefully this time next week six people would each have a new, functioning kidney. She knew how much this meant to the families involved. She'd been one of those families herself.

Now she needed to organise a team meeting. Initially she'd had three of the twelve surgeries scheduled to take place here, at the Kirribilli General Hospital, but now she had a fourth, which meant she needed a fourth surgical team—two for the organ retrievals and two more to complete the organ transplants.

Finally, she made a call to the hospital's PR division. This would be a big story and some media coverage could be a huge benefit to the drive to encourage organ donation. If they pulled it off.

There was no if, she told herself. They *had* to do this. There was too much at stake for it not to work. It *had* to be a success.

Grace fought to subdue the swarm of butterflies that was taking flight in her belly as she stood out in front of the Kirribilli General and faced a barrage of television cameras and media crews. The countdown had begun.

The transplant surgeries were scheduled to begin tomorrow morning at eight, in just over seventeen hours' time, but first there was a media statement to be made. She wasn't alone, she was flanked by numerous members of the renal transplant unit and the hospital's public relations department. It was a glorious sunny afternoon and the media had turned out in force. Grace didn't know if it was because it was a slow news day or if they really were interested in the story. She hoped it was the latter. This was a fabulous opportunity for some good publicity and a chance to raise organ donor awareness.

She took a deep breath and tried to calm her nerves as the hospital's PR spokesperson introduced Professor Elliot Martin, the head of the renal transplant unit. Elliot would introduce the other nephrologists and then it would be Grace's turn to speak. Public speaking was *so* not her thing. She didn't mind talking to the doctors, liaising with other transplant co-ordinators, and even talking to the patients' families about death and organ donation. That she could handle, but ask her to stand up in front of a group of strangers, well that was a whole different ball game. And strangers with cameras and microphones were even worse. She'd been taking classes and learning a few tricks. She knew her topic so she didn't need to be nervous but knowing that and convincing her autonomic nervous system of that fact were two different things.

Peering over the shoulder of the person standing in front of her and scanning the crowd, her gaze landed on Lola—her friend, colleague and flatmate. Lola had given her some advice this morning and as she caught her eye, Lola mimed undoing the top button of her uniform and gave her a wink. Grace bit back a smile. Lola's advice had been to imagine the crowd naked—apparently that was supposed to make them less intimidating.

She flicked her gaze away from Lola before her friend revealed anything she shouldn't on national television and before Grace herself burst out laughing. She continued to scan the crowd but it consisted mostly of middle-aged men, doctors and hospital administration staff, all approximately twenty years older than her twenty-seven years, and not anyone she wanted to picture naked.

Whoa, hang on a minute. Her eyes had skimmed the crowd but something, or rather someone, had caught her attention, and she quickly reversed her gaze.

On the opposite side of the crowd, right at the front, stood a man she wouldn't mind seeing naked.

He was tall, easily over six feet, and his shoulders were broad and his chest solid, yet he seemed to balance lightly on his feet. Despite his size he looked calm and centred and relaxed and she wished she had a tenth of his composure.

His dark hair was closely cropped and a designer two-day growth accentuated his oval face. He had a strong jaw and full lips beneath a narrow nose. His forehead was smooth and there was a slight furrow of concentration between his eyebrows that belied his relaxed stance. His dark eyes looked brooding and serious but that didn't detract from his looks in the slightest. He was incredibly handsome but that wasn't the only thing that had captured her attention. It was the contrast between him and everyone else around him. It was more than his height and his perfectly shaped face and symmetrical features. All of this was enhanced by his coffee-coloured skin, making him different enough to stand out from the crowd.

He wore a steel-blue suit with a white shirt that highlighted his complexion. His suit fitted perfectly and was impeccably tailored and pressed. He looked like he took pride in his appearance, and when you looked that good, why wouldn't you? He was delicious.

There was something vaguely familiar about him but surely that was just her imagination? She'd remember if she'd met him before, he was not someone who would be easily forgotten. It must be one of those déjà vu things, she decided as a flutter of lust rolled in her belly, competing with the butterflies.

She ran her gaze down the length of his suit jacket, taking note of his lean hips and powerful thighs. He was *definitely* someone she wouldn't mind seeing naked. She pictured him shrugging out of his jacket and loosening the buttons on his shirt, her mind completely absorbed by the mental image she was painting until she realised she couldn't recall a word of her speech.

Focus, focus, she told herself, but it was impossible to picture him getting naked *and* remember her speech.

She averted her gaze and caught Lola grinning at her, eyebrows raised. She dropped her eyes before her friend could make her laugh and focused on her breathing, hoping no one else had caught her ogling this glorious stranger.

Marcus could scarcely believe his good fortune. He'd arrived at Kirribilli General Hospital on an exchange programme from Western Australia to spend twelve weeks as a visiting specialist with the transplant unit and found that he was just in time to take part in a multiple paired kidney exchange operation. This was *exactly* why he was here. He'd always avoided returning to the east coast but Kirribilli General was the leading hospital in renal transplants and had pioneered the paired kidney exchange programme.

He'd been in two minds about whether to accept this posting before finally deciding that it was something he needed to do. The opportunity had been too good to pass up, given that he was advocating for the Queen Victoria Hospital in Perth to become involved in the programme too. It stood to reason that he should spend some time in Sydney getting first-hand knowledge.

He looked around at the media throng that

was gathered in front of the hospital. He realised that this was a big news story and he appreciated the fact that the hospital's PR division and the transplant team wanted to grab the opportunity for promotion but he could do without the circus. He itched to get going. He wanted to be in the operating theatre, with a scalpel in his hand. That was the one place where he always felt in control. Any surprises could be dealt with in a calm and clinical manner. He knew he had the skills to handle anything that could be thrown his way in Theatre. He'd spent years honing his skills. He liked to have control and being a surgeon afforded him that. Control and respect.

Elliot Martin, the head of the renal transplant unit, was speaking. Marcus knew he would be introducing the surgical teams soon and he returned his attention to his new boss, not wanting to miss his introduction.

He was excited. This was exactly the sort of opportunity he'd hoped to establish on his return to Perth and to get to be involved so early on was ideal.

He appreciated his good fortune and hoped

that, rather than just observing the kidney exchanges, his surgical skills would be required due to the number of operations that were being scheduled. He breathed deeply as he thought of how it would feel to be offered the opportunity to conduct one of the surgeries himself. If it happened, it would most likely be one of the retrievals but he didn't mind. He just wanted to be involved. Just wanted a chance to showcase his ability. It was one of the few things he knew he excelled at. And a retrieval was still a surgical procedure. It was a little more routine than a transplant but the margins for error were small and it was still an important process.

Doing a retrieval meant he would be removing a healthy kidney from a healthy person, which really contradicted the medical charter of 'Do no harm' but, in this case, he believed in the cause, in the greater good such a procedure would mean. He believed in this case that the benefits outweighed the disadvantages. The improved quality of life the selfless donor was offering to an unknown recipient was an amazing gift, although he still found it incredible that people were willing to sacrifice one of their organs, to offer it to a stranger, in return for one of their own loved ones receiving the same gift.

He couldn't imagine loving someone that much.

He refocused, tuning back in to Elliot's speech just in time to hear his introduction.

'I would like to introduce you all to Dr Janet Hosking and Dr Marcus Washington from the Queen Victoria Hospital in Western Australia, who are joining the Kirribilli General renal unit for the next three months.'

He stepped forward as his name was announced and his gaze landed on a petite redhead who was standing to Elliot's left but had previously been hidden from view behind someone else's shoulder. She was staring at him with her mouth open. Her heart-shaped face was pale, her skin smooth and creamy but her lips were painted a bright red, almost the same colour as her fiery copper hair. He'd only seen hair that colour once before in his life.

That couldn't be right. There had to be millions of people with that colour hair in the world.

Maybe he was mistaken. It had been twenty years ago after all. His memory had to be misleading him. Surely this couldn't be the same girl? What were the chances of that?

But the coil of fear in his gut told him that the chances were high. It was just his luck.

CHAPTER TWO

THE GORGEOUS MAN with amazing bone structure stepped forward and Grace's heart skipped a beat and her mouth dropped open.

Marcus Washington.

She could not believe it.

It had to be him. Even though he no longer resembled the twelve-year-old boy she'd once known, it *had* to be him. There couldn't be two of him.

He was a doctor? A nephrologist?

She hadn't thought about him for years but if she had she never would have imagined he would become a doctor. She knew that sounded harsh and judgemental but what she remembered of Marcus did not fit with her image of someone who had clearly ended up in a position of responsibility and service to others.

But what did she really know about him? She

had only been seven years old. What had she known about anything?

Her father was a doctor and, at the age of seven, everything she'd known or thought had been influenced by what and who she'd seen around her. Particularly by her own family. And Marcus's family had been about as different from hers as a seven-year-old could have imagined. But she knew enough now to understand that it wasn't about where you came from or what opportunities you were handed in life, but about what you did with those opportunities, those chances. It was about the choices you made. The drive and the desire to be the best that you could be.

She would never have pictured Marcus as a doctor but now here he was, standing in front of her looking polished, professional and perfect. It had to be him.

Grace knew a lot could change in twenty years and by the look of him, a lot had.

She was still staring at him, trying to make sense of what was happening, when he looked in her direction and caught her eye. Grace blushed and, cursing her fair skin, the bane of a redhead, she looked away as his gaze continued on over her. She finally remembered to close her mouth and hoped her reaction hadn't been captured on camera.

Had he recognised her?

It didn't appear so but, then, why would he? She was nothing like the seven-year-old he had last seen.

She must have missed an earlier HR announcement about him coming to her hospital. She would have remembered if she'd seen his name. What had Elliot said? He would be here for three months? Attached to her department?

She swivelled her eyes and observed him through the curtain of her hair as he shook Elliot's hand. She took a second look. And a third. She had changed in the intervening years but so had he. There was nothing left of the skinny adolescent in him. Nothing at all.

Not that she was complaining. He looked just fine.

His dark hair was close cropped now, his wild curls a distant memory. And where had those broad shoulders and powerful legs come from? Her last memory of him had been as a tall and thin pre-teen with skinny brown legs in shorts that had always looked as if he'd outgrown them. That boy was gone now. Replaced by a taller, more muscular, more confident and far better dressed adult version.

She didn't need to see him naked to imagine the toned, muscular body that was under the suit. She had always thought he was exotic in a slightly out-of-place way, but he appeared to have grown into his skin. She'd never known his mother but she'd heard she was Caribbean or something if she remembered correctly, and the mixture of her genes with Marcus's Caucasian father had combined to give Marcus the best of both worlds. And that had never been more obvious than today.

But the one thing that hadn't changed was that the adult Marcus was not paying her any attention. Just like the adolescent one. He had kept to himself as a child. It had seemed he'd never paid *anyone* any attention. Maybe he'd been trying not to draw attention to himself. He had been different from the other kids at school, different in looks and different in his background, and Grace knew that had made him a target for some of the other children. It didn't pay to be different when you were a kid. It didn't pay to stand out from the crowd.

But looking at him now it appeared that things had improved for him in the intervening twenty years. He still stood out from the crowd but now there was a sense of strength and confidence about him. All traces of the shy, quiet, reclusive child had been wiped out.

Grace was curious to know where he'd been, what had happened to him, but her questions would have to wait. It was almost her turn to speak and she needed to get her head back in the present. She was still new in this job and it was important to make a good impression. She couldn't afford to be distracted by the past. No matter how good it looked.

She picked Lola out in the crowd. That was a mistake too. Lola had obviously seen Grace's reaction to Marcus and was grinning wildly. At least she didn't know the full story. Grace glared at her and looked for someone else in the crowd to focus on as she tried to ignore Marcus, who had stepped back with the other nephrologists. He was no longer front and centre, but that didn't stop Grace from being totally aware of him. She imagined she could feel his presence even though she kept her eyes averted from him.

She took a deep breath and stepped up to the microphone as Elliot introduced her.

'As you know,' she addressed the crowd, 'we have four surgeries scheduled here tomorrow, which would not be possible without the generous gift of organs from family and friends of those in need.'

Her job today was to raise awareness about organ donation and, somehow, she managed to get through her spiel and ignore Marcus, even though she could feel his eyes on her. Most of the eyes in the crowd were on her but she could feel Marcus's piercing gaze more than most. There was an intensity about it and she knew she couldn't afford to look his way. She'd definitely lose her train of thought.

'The majority of Australians are willing donors,' she continued, 'so the problem we have is not a lack of interest but a lack of knowledge coupled with a lack of suitable organs. We need suitable organs and then we need permission to use those organs. If your family don't know your wishes or don't support your decision, we cannot use your organs. But, in some cases, living organ donations are a possibility and that is the case for the surgeries we have scheduled for tomorrow.

'All these surgeries are part of the paired kidney exchange, where living donors are giving up a kidney to a stranger in exchange for a better matched kidney for a loved one in need. There are twelve surgeries scheduled across the country, which makes it the largest paired exchange exercise ever conducted in Australia.

'Transplants using organs donated by the living have a higher success rate and you can imagine the freedom that this will afford someone—no more dialysis and fewer hospital visits. So thank you to those wonderful donors who are giving not just a kidney but the gift of a better life.

'If you are interested in finding out more there is further information on the organ donation website, but *please* also remember to talk about this issue to your families and let them know your wishes in this very important matter.'

Grace stepped gratefully back into her place after her speech and planned to bolt as soon as the media questions ended but Elliot called her name as she turned to flee. She stopped in her tracks and took a deep breath. She knew what he wanted. He wanted to introduce her to the two new doctors. Only they weren't both new to her.

She wondered if Marcus would remember her.

She pasted a smile on her face and turned around. Sure enough, Elliot was standing between Janet and Marcus. Grace tried to take control and introduced herself to Janet first, shaking her hand before looking up at Marcus.

He towered over her. Grace was tiny, only five feet two inches tall. Away from the hospital she liked to wear heels but they were impractical with all the running around she did and now, in her flat, sensible shoes, Marcus was easily a foot taller than her.

He stared down at her with a look that was

far from friendly. She could only assume he remembered her. And not fondly.

She didn't think she'd ever given him a reason to dislike her yet his jaw was clenched and tense and his lips were firmly closed. No welcoming smile there!

She remembered other kids teasing him. But she never had, she'd been too young, and she doubted that her brothers would have either, they hadn't been raised that way, but Marcus certainly didn't look pleased to see her. He looked as if he was daring her to say something about his past and she wondered what he thought she might say after all this time.

She couldn't actually remember him leaving town. One minute he had been there, living in Toowoomba, going to school with her brother. The next minute he'd gone. Vanished. Just like his mother before him.

But now here he was. Fighting fit, successful and gorgeous.

So what was the story? She was desperate to know.

She put out her hand, waiting to see if he

would say anything, wanting to know if he would divulge their shared past.

'Grace… Gibson, is it?'

You know damn well it is, she wanted to say, but the look in his eye stopped her short and made her hold her tongue. Which surprised her. Holding her tongue had never been her forte.

Her hand hovered in mid-air until Marcus's fingers curled around her palm. Perhaps he was just trying to make amends for his lack of manners but his touch flummoxed her. His tone was cool but his hand was warm. Warm enough to send fire through her fingertips. Her whole arm tingled and set her heart racing. Her breath caught in her throat and she barely remembered to nod her head in acknowledgement of his words.

What was he doing to her? How was he doing it? She was breathless, frozen to the spot, yet her body felt as if it was overheating. The colours around her intensified, making her feel dizzy, and sounds receded. She felt overloaded, as if her body couldn't cope with too many sensations at once. Marcus's touch was enough to cope with. More than enough.

What was wrong with her? She wondered if she was having a panic attack or if her system was shutting down. What had he done to her? She never lost her nerve.

She could feel another embarrassing rush of blood beginning to flood her body, only this time it wasn't in her face. This time it was starting somewhere south of that but she knew her face would soon be bright red also. She pulled her hand away, severing the contact.

Her hand was trembling. She was trembling.

She stuck her hand in her pocket to disguise her tremor and looked at her feet, unable to maintain eye contact.

If Marcus had been daring her to say something, he'd won the dare. She was completely tongue-tied.

Elliot was still talking, apparently oblivious to the feelings that were raging through Grace and completely unaware of the electric undercurrents flowing between her and his new colleague.

Perhaps it was all in her head, she thought, but she didn't really believe that.

'You've read the patient histories?' Elliot

asked, and Janet and Marcus nodded. 'Janet, I thought you could perform the kidney removal on Rosa. I will assist and, Marcus, you are more experienced, you can observe that surgery and then you will perform the transplant later.'

Grace had decided not to be such a coward and had lifted her eyes again now that the attention was off her and she saw Marcus's small double take. He looked surprised by Elliot's words—had he not been expecting that?

Elliot continued speaking. 'Grace will have any other information you might need pre-op. If there's anything more you need, you can liaise with her. I will do the other transplant, with Janet assisting, and Andrew Murray will take care of the second organ retrieval. Your patients were admitted first thing this morning—'

'Already?' Marcus interrupted.

Grace knew it was unusual. Normally patients were admitted as late as possible, sometimes only on the day of surgery, mostly as a cost-saving exercise, but she'd advocated strongly that admission be brought forward.

Elliot nodded. 'Grace thought it would be

prudent to get them admitted early to avoid the media circus that we're anticipating, and I agreed. We don't want to increase their stress levels by having reporters jostling for a comment as they arrive, and this also means we don't have to worry about traffic delays and other things that might be out of our control tomorrow.'

Marcus looked at Grace. She thought he might be about to say something and she wondered if it would have been complimentary but his expression remained guarded. Janet had no reservations. 'Great, I'll go and introduce myself to Rosa.'

Elliot moved away and Janet and Marcus followed him without a backward glance. Grace stood and watched them go. Had he forgotten about her already?

She watched as his long strides quickly put distance between them. Her legs were incapable of moving. Her knees were still shaky and she felt light-headed. She stood still and took a couple of deep breaths, getting the air back into her lungs, remembering to breathe as she sorted through her mental list of tasks ahead of her.

She had plenty to do before tomorrow. Final physical checks of their patients had to be co-ordinated, she had to confirm the courier ar-rangements and continue discussions with the other renal co-ordinators in Brisbane, Mel-bourne and North Sydney hospitals. She had a lot of balls in the air and she couldn't afford to drop any. She couldn't afford to worry about Marcus Washington and about what he was thinking or where he'd been for the last twenty years. There were far too many more important things waiting to occupy her time.

But that didn't stop her from immediately racing back to her office and checking her emails. There must have been one announc-ing the three-month appointment of Janet and Marcus. She couldn't believe she'd missed it. She typed Marcus's name into the search func-tion and hit enter. An email from a month ago popped up. The heading gave no clue as to who the doctors were, and she was certain that if it had included his name that would have caught her eye. It was also in amongst dozens of emails relating to the paired kidney exchange, which would explain why she'd skimmed over it without even opening it.

She opened it now. She was eager to see what information it gave her.

She ignored Janet's CV and clicked on the file pertaining to Marcus. He had graduated from university in Western Australia. Had he moved there from Toowoomba? Why? Who had he gone to? Had his mother moved there? Was she alive? But if she was, why hadn't she taken him years before? Grace had more questions than answers.

She continued reading. He had spent some time in the US during his speciality years, returning to work in Perth. And now he was here. His career history was brief and, of course, there was no personal information included. Nothing to tell her if he was married, engaged, straight, gay—although she was pretty sure he was straight—or if he had a wife and kids back home in Perth.

She closed her email down. She didn't have time to do a wider search on him. She had all the final pieces of the transplant puzzle to put in place. She had dozens of phone calls to make, she needed to check in with the other hospitals to make sure that all their patients were still well enough to undergo surgery and that no one had changed their minds. One hiccup could ruin the whole exercise.

She was glad she'd made arrangements for her patients to be admitted early. As Elliot had outlined, her reasons were valid. There were enough other logistical arrangements to be made once the kidneys had been harvested, without adding to the complications with things going haywire prior to the surgeries. It would only take one problem to snowball and potentially disrupt all the surgeries, and she wanted everything to run smoothly.

By the time she ended her final call to one of the Melbourne hospitals it was dusk outside. She should have clocked off but there was still more to do. Her schedule didn't stick to regular nursing shifts any more, not since she'd become the renal co-ordinator. Her shifts supposedly ran from nine to five but it was not often that she stuck to those hours. Transplant patients could receive news day or night and she was often called back into the hospital to speak to the families of donors and to the transplant recipients. Plus, she had no reason to race out the door at the end of the day. She had nothing to race home for. No significant other, no children, no pets. If it wasn't for work, her life would be a bit empty.

She switched off her office lights but, still in no hurry to leave, she thought she'd check one last time on the four patients waiting for surgery.

She got two patients with her first visit.

'Gentlemen, how are you feeling?'

She greeted Rob and Paul, two brothers, one a donor, the other a recipient. Rob's donated kidney was going to Brisbane in exchange for a kidney for his brother, as unfortunately their tissue types didn't match. They were sitting together, chatting, when Grace entered Paul's room. They seemed quite relaxed but Paul had been through this before so it was nothing new for him. His first kidney transplant, from a deceased donor, had lasted twenty-five years but was failing now. It was wonderful to think that the paired exchange programme could hopefully give him another shot at a successful transplant.

As Grace chatted to the two men she quickly revised her opinion of how they were feeling. Paul seemed far more relaxed than Rob.

'Are you ready for tomorrow, Rob?' she asked gently when Paul went to the bathroom, leaving the two of them alone for a moment.

'I was told that the research shows that kidney disease most commonly affects both kidneys, is that right?'

'That does seem to be the case. You're worried about your remaining kidney?' Rob's nerves were not unusual in Grace's experience. The donor was often more on edge than the recipient. Grace didn't know if it was fear of the unknown or a lack of experience with hospitals or the fact that the donor wasn't actually sick but was giving up a perfectly healthy organ. Rob was going from being a healthy, intact individual to one who would be minus an organ. Granted, he could do without it but that was assuming his remaining kidney continued to function normally. Hence his question. She knew he'd heard these answers before but her role as co-ordinator was often as much about counselling as co-ordinating.

'We don't anticipate problems, Rob,' she re-assured him when he nodded. 'We wouldn't let you do this if we thought it could create problems for you down the track.'

'There's no way I'm backing out,' he empha-sised firmly, 'and my kidney only has to last long enough to see me out.'

'Okay. Get some rest and I'll see you in the morning.'

Grace made her way to Rosa's room across the hall next. Rosa's kidney would be going to Paul, not that either of them were privy to that piece of information, in exchange for a kid-ney for Rosa's son in Melbourne. Despite being across the corridor from each other, Paul and Rosa wouldn't meet.

Rosa was sitting beside her bed, knitting, the television on low volume. She was a widow with just the one son living interstate and Grace knew she was used to spending quiet nights alone. She'd told Grace she was fine as long as her hands were busy and she liked to knit. She seemed calm and only had a couple of questions for Grace, both of which had to do with her son's prognosis. Rosa wasn't worried about herself at all.

'We have excellent results with kidney transplants,' Grace told her again, happy to answer her questions. 'Especially with living organ donors. Most kidneys will last ten years and some as long as twenty-five.' She wished she could tell Rosa that her kidney was going to Paul and that he was one of the people whose first transplanted kidney had lasted twenty-five years but she couldn't divulge that information, even though she knew it would make Rosa feel better. She said goodnight before popping into Connie's room, her last stop for the evening.

'Hey, Connie.'

Connie was the recipient of the spare kidney and even though in testing it had proved to be a good match there was a little bit of the unknown associated with this one, given the unexpectedness of the windfall, and Grace knew Connie was nervous.

Connie had moved to Sydney from the country eighteen months ago to have regular dialysis. She suffered from autosomal dominant polycystic kidney disease and Grace knew she was finding things difficult. She was only able to work part time and her support group of friends and family were not close by.

Because of her illness and medical appointments her social life was limited and Grace knew that this transplant would make a huge difference to her quality of life. Grace's sister-in-law had suffered from the same disease and had undergone a transplant five years ago, so Grace knew from personal experience how different Connie's life could potentially be. Connie was only twenty-seven, the same age as Grace, and because of that and her circumstances Grace felt a deeper affinity for her than for some of her other patients.

'Where is everyone?' Grace asked as she looked around. Although they weren't compatible donors, Connie's family were providing support to her in other ways, and when Grace stepped into the room she was surprised to find that Connie didn't have company. She knew her parents had come to the city to be with Connie for the surgery and the recovery.

'Mum and Dad will be back later, they've just gone to get some dinner.'

'How are you doing?' she asked as she flicked through Connie's chart, pleased to see everything looked stable and normal.

'I'm not worried about the operation. Just worried about what will happen if it doesn't work. I really want to be able to have kids. I need this to go well.'

Grace knew pregnancy was not out of the question for Connie if the transplant was successful but, as that was an unknown at this point, she couldn't make any promises. Who knew what would happen? The only thing you could do in life was to hope for the best. All they could do in this situation was hope the kidney was a viable, healthy and suitable match for Connie. And no one could control any of that. It wasn't her place to promise Connie things she might not be able to deliver.

'Have you spoken to Dr Washington about this?'

'OMG,' Connie gushed, 'thank you so much.'

Grace frowned. Connie's train of thought had clearly gone off at a complete tangent to the discussion Grace had thought they were having. 'What for?'

'Dr Washington. He is *hot*.'

Grace wasn't surprised that Connie had noticed Marcus, as he was difficult to miss, but she did *not* want to have this conversation. It felt inappropriate, even though she knew it was just chatter. She didn't want to talk about Marcus but she wasn't sure why. 'Seriously? You're about to have major surgery and you're thinking about your surgeon?'

Connie grinned. 'Thinking about him is proving to be a good distraction.'

'I guess I can see your point.' Grace could understand the fascination but she didn't have time to discuss Marcus's myriad attributes. She didn't know if she could be completely complimentary. 'But I really can't discuss him.'

'I just wish I didn't have to be asleep when he operates on me,' Connie sighed. 'He is totally gorgeous. Do you know if he's single?'

Grace had no idea. 'You know it's against the rules for doctors to get romantically involved with their patients, right?'

'I won't always be his patient.'

'He's only in Sydney for a few weeks. He's from Perth and once you get through tomorrow you will need to focus on your recovery, not chase after your surgeon.'

'But it would give me something to look forward to.'

This conversation was making Grace feel uncomfortable. She needed to end it. She turned her attention to a box of medical supplies that didn't need tidying but which gave her something to focus on. 'You shouldn't be getting excited, you need to keep your blood pressure stable,' she commented as she shuffled and sorted the small packets of wipes and dressings.

'What's this about your BP? It's not raised, is it?'

Grace had her back to the door and the sound of Marcus's voice made her jump. She didn't need to see him; his voice was already instantly recognisable. Deep, quiet and purposeful, it was a voice that commanded attention. When he spoke you wanted to listen. At least, she did. Grace turned and caught the tell-tale sign of a blush sweeping over Connie's cheeks as she greeted her surgeon.

'Nothing. It's all good,' Grace replied hastily.

Marcus swivelled his gaze to her but said nothing. He picked up Connie's chart and flicked through her records.

Grace bristled. Didn't he believe her? Not that she'd checked Connie's blood pressure herself but she *had* checked the chart. 'I am a registered nurse as well as the transplant co-ordinator,' she told him, deciding to give him the benefit of the doubt. Perhaps he wasn't aware of her qualifications. She'd only been the transplant co-ordinator for a few months but she was medically qualified and was gaining valuable experience all the time.

His gaze was cool and assessing when he looked at her again, his brown eyes imperturbable. He nodded once, but made no comment.

What was wrong with him? Did he have no warmth? Grace wondered, but then she recalled how her skin had burned when he'd held her hand. There was warmth in his touch but it was a pity it didn't appear to extend to his character.

He put Connie's chart away and perched on the edge of her bed and Grace watched as Connie's eyes nearly popped out of her head.

'Any last questions for me before I see you in the morning?' He smiled at his patient and Grace felt an unexpected stab of jealousy. His smile was incredible, transforming his features from striking and exotic to jaw-droppingly handsome, and she wished desperately that he would smile at her like that.

'Grace and I were just talking about what comes after the transplant. I really want to have children.'

Grace watched as Connie toyed with the ends of her hair and looked up at Marcus through her lashes. Was she flirting with him?

'If everything goes according to plan, pregnancy shouldn't be an issue after a transplant but it is recommended, and I certainly encourage my patients to follow this advice, to wait one year to ensure the transplant is functioning as we'd like and that your medications are stable.'

'That's okay. That will give me time to find a boyfriend.'

Yep, she was definitely flirting. She was all fluttering eyelashes and rosy cheeks. She certainly didn't look like a person who was critically ill and about to undergo major surgery. Not that Grace could blame her. Marcus was gorgeous, but if he noticed Connie's attempts to entice him, he didn't take the bait.

'You will need close monitoring during a pregnancy,' he replied, leaving Connie's comment well alone, 'but you would be closely monitored anyway and we can discuss any other issues post-surgery.'

'Great. If that's all, we'll leave you to get some rest now,' Grace said, keen to usher Marcus out of the room before Connie could actually proposition him.

As Marcus stood and started to leave, Grace shot Connie a warning glance behind his back, but Connie just grinned and then laughed it off, making Grace smile back. At least she was in good spirits.

Grace followed Marcus out of the room. His strides were long and Grace found her gaze drawn to his hips. He'd removed his suit jacket, leaving the shape of his buttocks under his pants clearly defined as his legs ate up the length of the corridor. Grace forced herself to keep her eyes lifted. She didn't want to be caught ogling him or running into something because her attention was elsewhere.

She got the feeling he was trying to put as much distance between them as possible. But she had no idea why. Her curiosity got the better of her and she hurried after him. She wanted to know what his issue was. Why he was so abrupt with her. She didn't think she'd done anything to put him off, yet his aloofness was definitely directed at her. She had to admit he was an empathetic doctor with a good bedside manner and maybe she'd just have to be satisfied with that. But she still wanted some answers.

'Dr Washington!'

He stopped and turned towards her.

'Have I done something to upset you?' she asked as she caught up to him.

'No.'

Grace waited for him to elaborate but he didn't say another word. Man, he could totally be the poster boy for the strong, silent type.

Oh, well. Nothing ventured, nothing gained, she thought as she asked, 'Do you remember me?'

Marcus looked down at the petite redhead

standing in front of him. She had her hands on her hips and looked as if she'd like to tear him to shreds. 'What do you mean? Of course I do,' he replied, attempting to use his most reasonable tone in an attempt to calm her down. 'We were just in Connie's room and I only met you a few hours ago.'

'I meant from before.'

He watched her with his steady gaze but said nothing. He wasn't going to admit to anything. Not until he knew what she wanted. She reminded him of a firecracker about to explode.

'You grew up in Toowoomba,' she said. It was apparent she wasn't going to be intimidated and she certainly wasn't asking him a question. She looked small and easy to handle but, just like a firecracker, he got the impression that once something set her off, you'd know all about it and there'd be nowhere to hide. 'I lived around the corner from you. You were at school with my brothers, Lachlan and Hamish Gibson.'

It was obvious she knew who he was. He'd suspected as much. He had recognised her too. Well, not her face as such, but her hair matched with her name was a dead giveaway. Her striking copper locks were so distinctive. He hadn't *wanted* to think she was the same person even though it was blatantly clear she was, just as it was clear she remembered him.

He cursed his luck. 'Was I?'

He knew he was being bullish but he couldn't help it. He'd spent twenty years trying to get away from his past. Twenty years spent reinventing himself and wiping away all traces of his childhood. He hadn't been back to Toowoomba in all that time and he'd even debated the wisdom of returning to the east coast for this three-month stint but the opportunity of this experience at the Kirribilli General Hospital had been too good to refuse. Guilt and opportunity had brought him back. And now it seemed it was about to make him pay.

He hadn't expected to run into anyone from his past and he certainly wouldn't have expected to be remembered. He didn't want to remember who he had been and the life he'd lived then. He didn't want to think about it and he definitely didn't want to talk about it. So he stayed silent, refusing to incriminate himself by admitting any recollection. He couldn't admit

to Grace that he had lied. That he *had* recognised her.

'I guess I look a bit different,' Grace admitted when he stayed mute. 'I must only have
been about seven the last time I would have
seen you.'

Was there a question in there? Was she wondering why he'd never come back? Had she
even noticed?

He wasn't going to respond to vague insin-
uations but she was right. She looked nothing like he remembered. He remembered her
brothers and he remembered their little sister
with skinned knees and missing teeth. The only
thing that remained of the seven-year-old she'd
once been was her hair. Her fiery copper locks
hung in loose waves over her shoulders, its rich
colour bright and vibrant against the contrast
of her navy uniform. He'd hadn't seen a colour
like it since leaving Toowoomba.

But everything else about her was different.
She no longer looked like anyone's kid sister.
She had filled out in all the right places. She
was tiny, a good foot shorter than his six feet
two inches, but her proportions were perfect.

Her shirt was tucked into navy trousers, pants which would have been unflattering on most figures, yet his eye was drawn to her small waist, the swell of her breasts and the curve of her hips. He felt an unexpected surge of lust. Bloody hell, that was inappropriate. He lifted his head and met her amber eyes. They blazed at him. She appeared to have the fiery temper to match her hair but what was getting her so riled up? Had she noticed his inappropriate once-over? He needed to douse the flames of her temper and make sure he didn't set her off completely. Something told him there would be no stopping her if he did that.

Or maybe he should take up the challenge he could see in her eyes. She gave off an air of not being one to back down. Of having the courage of her convictions. That didn't appear to have changed. He remembered more about her than he cared to admit. She'd been loud and boisterous, full of energy; he'd always known when she was around and he suspected that hadn't changed in twenty years. He wondered what had.

The idea of putting a flame to her wick just to

see what would happen was strangely exciting but he resisted the temptation. He didn't want to bring unnecessary attention to the two of them. He didn't want anyone asking awkward questions. Going under the radar was always best. He'd learnt that from experience.

But what did she want? What was she after? What did she remember of him? What secrets could she spill?

He hoped not many.

As a child he'd been quiet, shy and nervous. The complete antithesis to Grace. He'd been nervous around the kids at school and nervous around his father. His life had been unpredictable and devoid of routine but it hadn't been until he'd been at boarding school as a teenager that he'd realised that not everyone's lives were like that. He'd never experienced anything different. Most of the time he'd just tried to get from morning to evening without being noticed. It had seemed his presence had irritated people—his classmates and his father—and he had never been sure about what was going to happen, how people were going to react to him, although more often than not it had been unfavourably. He'd learnt to keep his head down, to try to be inconspicuous, but that had never been easy when he'd looked so different.

Thanks to his Caribbean mother he wasn't white but he wasn't indigenous either. He was part black but not the black that was common in Toowoomba. There wasn't another person in the town who had the same genetic mix as him and, if that wasn't enough to make him stand out, his family history and his unorthodox father had certainly made sure that everyone had singled him out.

His mother had disappeared when he'd been six, leaving him behind with a father who had chosen to develop a relationship with alcohol instead of with his son. His young life had been full of disappointments and he'd learnt early on not to ask for or expect much, and that the only person he could count on not to let him down was himself.

He'd been determined to escape a miserable childhood and to avoid all memories of his past. He'd worked hard over many years to forget who he was and where he came from. He didn't want to be remembered as that boy. That wasn't him any more.

And he didn't want anyone to remind him of it either.

Which made Grace the last person he wanted to see.

CHAPTER THREE

'I DON'T REMEMBER you from then,' he told her as he shook his head, but Grace knew he was lying.

She just didn't know why. Did he think he was above her now that he was a surgeon or was it for a more personal reason? He'd been perfectly pleasant to Connie. Not warm exactly but he was her surgeon and he certainly hadn't brushed her aside like he'd tried to do with *her*.

His dark brown eyes challenged her to say something more and for a moment she was tempted to but something stopped her. She couldn't have said what it was, and it was most unlike her to back down from an argument, but she had a sudden sense that she would regret the words that were itching to come out of her mouth so she bit down on her lip and kept quiet.

And Marcus turned and walked away.

Clearly the conversation was over and this

time she didn't follow him. For some reason he seemed to have an issue with her. She didn't want it to be personal but, whatever it was, she wouldn't let it lie. But it would wait for another day. She returned to her office and collected her bag before heading to Billi's Bar.

As usual the bar was crowded with hospital staff. It was just across the road from the hospital and the staff kept it well patronised. She waved to Gary, who was serving customers, but made her way through the crowd, searching for Lola. She hadn't intended on calling into the bar tonight but she needed to vent her frustration. She wasn't sure why she was frustrated and that only made matters worse. Why did she care that Marcus was lying to her? Why did she care that he said he didn't remember her?

She found Lola towards the back of the room. She smiled in greeting but was looking over Grace's shoulder.

'Who are you looking for?' Grace asked.

'I thought you might bring the hot doc with you.'

Grace didn't need to ask who Lola was referring to but it had taken less time than she'd expected for the conversation to turn to Marcus. Was he all people could talk about? First Connie and now Lola.

'I'm the last person he would want to have a drink with.'

'Why? You haven't upset him already, have you?'

Lola's comment was not without merit. Grace knew she'd upset people before with her quick temper and tongue, but in Marcus's case she couldn't think of what she could have possibly done to make him behave so distantly towards her. She sighed and dumped her bag on the table then retrieved her phone. She needed to keep it handy as with so many surgeries scheduled for tomorrow she couldn't afford to miss a call. 'No,' she replied, 'but I don't think he likes me.'

Lola frowned. 'How can he not like you? He doesn't even know you.'

'So he says.'

'What does that mean?'

She pulled out a stool and sat down. She needed to debrief. 'He grew up in Toowoomba.

He went to school with Lachlan and Hamish but he says he doesn't remember me.'

Lola laughed.

'What's so funny?' Grace's nerves were already frayed and having Lola laugh at her only irritated her more.

'You're upset because he doesn't remember you.'

'No, I'm upset because he's lying to me. He lived just around the corner from us. I used to walk past his house every day.'

'Was he there?'

Grace actually had no idea. She remembered walking past his house because it had always spooked her. The memory from years ago was still vivid in her mind but Lola was right. She couldn't actually remember if Marcus had been in there. She shrugged and admitted, 'I don't know.'

'Was he friends with your brothers?'

'Not really.' From what she could remember, he hadn't really been friends with anyone. She couldn't remember seeing him with friends. She thought he had played rugby but she could be imagining that.

'So maybe he really doesn't remember you. When did you see him last?'

'He left when I was about seven, so he would have been twelve. I haven't seen him since.'

'That's years ago! You can't blame him if he's forgotten you.'

But Grace didn't think she was wrong. She was certain he remembered her. There was something she couldn't put her finger on but she knew he wasn't telling her the truth.

'Where did he go when he left Toowoomba?' Lola asked.

'I have no idea. He just disappeared.'

'The whole family?'

Grace shook her head. 'No, just him. His father was still there.' Grace realised she hadn't thought about Mr Washington for years and she couldn't remember the last time she'd seen him either. Was he in a nursing home? Dead? She wouldn't have been surprised. Marcus's old house had been bulldozed after Grace had moved to Sydney and a new one was now in its place. With another family in it. But she had no idea what had happened to Marcus's father.

'So he left with his mother?'

'No. I never knew his mother. She disappeared years before.'

Lola leant forward, resting her elbows on the table. 'So his mother left suddenly, and then him? That sounds intriguing.'

'I really don't know much about it.'

There had been plenty of rumours about the family. Grace had grown up hearing them and then when Marcus had disappeared as well, the rumours had only intensified. The most popular theory amongst the kids at school had been that Marcus's father was responsible for the disappearances. They'd said he'd killed his wife and then he'd killed Marcus. As a seven-year-old that had frightened Grace immensely, and because of those stories it was unlikely she'd ever forget about Marcus Washington. The story of his disappearance had become an urban myth. The kids had been fascinated by it and Grace's imagination had led her to not only believe the stories but to embellish all sorts of gory details.

Her parents had told her and her brothers that Marcus had gone to live with his aunt but at the age of seven she'd put that story in the same category as the one about the fate of their pet roosters. Her parents had told her that the roosters were sent away to live on a farm because they were happier there, but her brothers had gleefully informed her that they really ended up in someone's pot with their heads chopped off. Grace feared Marcus had met the same fate and that her parents were lying to protect her because, surely, if he had gone to live with his aunt he would still come back to visit his father. And he never did. In Grace's seven-year-old brain this meant the rumours must be true. Marcus was dead.

It wasn't hard for her to believe the rumours and to imagine that Mr Washington had somehow played a hand in the disappearance of his family. When they were never seen again that story made sense. And, in Grace's young opinion, Marcus's father was a strange man. Walking past Marcus's house had always spooked her and after his disappearance things had only got worse. The house had been untidy and unloved. Paint had been peeling off the woodwork, the iron roof rusty and the front garden overgrown with weeds. If it hadn't been for the fact that Mr Washington had often sat or slept on an old sofa on the front veranda you would have thought the house had been abandoned. He'd always looked dishevelled and, if she saw him on his feet, unsteady.

She'd had to walk past the house on her way to and from school and after Marcus's disappearance she had *always* crossed to the opposite side of the road just in case Mr Washington was out the front. Lachlan, who was then twelve, had told her not to be ridiculous. He'd insisted that if Marcus's dad had killed him he'd be locked up, not wandering the streets, but Grace had remained wary for many years until she'd been old enough to understand Lachlan's logic and recognise the rumours for what they were.

Later she'd understood that Marcus's father had been an alcoholic but at the age of seven she hadn't got any of that. When she'd learned the truth she'd then wondered what had made him drink. Had it been losing his wife and son that had done that to him?

But Grace didn't share her thoughts with Lola. Normally she wouldn't hesitate to gossip with her but something about this felt wrong.

Obviously Marcus hadn't been murdered and all her thoughts were based on rumour and supposition. She was sorry she'd brought up the topic now. She recalled the look in Marcus's eyes. The look that she'd thought had been daring her to say something. Maybe it hadn't been a challenge but fear? Was he afraid of what she might say about him?

What could she possibly say? What did he think she knew?

Did it matter? Even imagining she had tales to tell could be enough. She knew what that was like. After her boyfriend had taken his own life Grace had felt the eyes of a small town on her. Mostly the town had been supportive of her and her grief after Johnny's death but she'd still felt horribly exposed. That had been one reason why she'd wanted to leave Toowoomba. Too many people knew too much about her. She knew what it felt like when others made assumptions about you. How it felt when things you'd rather keep to yourself were discussed in public.

Was that what Marcus was worried about? That she would reveal his secrets?

But what did she know about him? What *could* she know about him when she hadn't seen or heard anything about him for twenty years?

Nothing.

The truth of the matter was it wasn't her story to tell and she was sorry she and Lola had even been discussing him. She knew he wouldn't like it and for some reason that bothered her. She picked up her bag and tucked her phone inside it. 'I should go,' she said. 'I have a big day tomorrow.'

Grace was at the hospital bright and early the following morning. She had checked on her patients and found them in varying degrees of anxiety but otherwise okay. She'd contacted the renal transplant co-ordinators at the other hospitals, double-checking and making sure there were no last-minute problems, and now she was heading for the conference room to prepare her notes in anticipation of the doctors' meeting that was scheduled for half past seven to have a final run-through of the day's proceedings.

She scrolled through the messages on her

phone, making sure again that she hadn't missed anything important as she waited for everyone to arrive. Elliot was first, followed by Janet and then Marcus. She wasn't watching the door but she knew the minute Marcus entered the room. She looked up to find him watching her. Was that what she could sense? The feeling of being watched? No, it was more than that. Her body recognised him. Her body responded to his proximity. But she suspected she was being fanciful. It was nothing more than an awareness of an extremely good-looking man. Who had absolutely no time for her.

He didn't hold her gaze. Didn't acknowledge her in any way. He didn't smile. Or nod. He gave her nothing and she was disappointed. He greeted his colleagues as he found himself a seat but he did not make eye contact with her again. Was that deliberate or not? She wanted him to like her but she got an uneasy sense that something about her irritated him and that bothered her. She wanted him to like her but right now she didn't have time to think about why that might be. She lowered her eyes and looked over her notes. She refused to waste any more time wondering about Marcus. She was just as capable of ignoring him as he was of her.

She listened as Elliot ran everyone through the day's schedule. He was following the notes she had written on the whiteboard as soon as she'd confirmed every patient's status and he checked a couple of minor details with her. The surgeries were scheduled to commence at eight o'clock with concurrent harvesting of the kidneys. The donor patients were being prepped for surgery as he spoke and once Grace received confirmation that every patient was anaesthetised the surgeries would begin. The timing and, in a way, the success of the surgeries depended on her. She controlled the process and she needed to focus.

The actual transplant timeline varied and was dependent on when the donated kidneys arrived at their respective hospitals. There was still a lot to co-ordinate and it was going to be a long day for her. She would be on deck until the last patient went to Recovery. She was the link not only between the surgeons and the hospitals but also between the patients and their families. It was going to be hectic but while she would co-ordinate the surgeries the actual outcomes of them would be out of her hands. It was almost over. The final day was here and all that was left for her to do was to continue to liaise and to watch and to hope. And to wait. She crossed her fingers and hoped the day would be successful.

The medical staff split into their surgical teams at the conclusion of the meeting and Grace headed for the observation gallery that overlooked two of the theatres. She watched as the patients were wheeled in, Rosa in one theatre to her left, Rob in the other. She would be able to communicate with the operating teams via an intercom and she waited and watched as the anaesthetists began their job. The surgeons hovered, gloved and gowned.

She held her mobile phone in her hand, waiting for the sound of incoming text messages and constantly scanning the screen to check she hadn't missed anything. She saw Rosa's eyes close as the anaesthetic took hold and then, one by one, the messages started coming in. One, two, three and four. She waited for confirmation from the two theatres in front of her before sending her own reply.

'All donors confirmed asleep.'

Until everyone was under anaesthetic there was always a chance that one or more donors could change their minds. But no one could back out now. The six harvesting surgeries could begin.

Grace waited again, holding her breath until she got confirmation that all surgeries had begun. She breathed out and sank into a seat behind the viewing glass. Technically she could watch both Rosa's and Rob's operations but she concentrated on Rosa's. That was where Marcus was. She had vowed to ignore him but her eyes were repeatedly drawn to him regardless of her decision.

He stood slightly back from the operating table as he was in Theatre as an observer only, watching Elliot and Janet operating, but Grace knew he was tall enough to see over the shoulders of the nurse who stood in front of him.

Janet and Elliot worked together. The surgery began as keyhole and Grace could watch proceedings on a monitor in the corner of the observation gallery. The kidneys were tucked up under the lower ribs and not always easy to access. The procedure was time consuming, requiring a steady hand and patience as the kidney needed to be carefully and precisely detached. All the important attachments needed to be preserved. Smaller blood vessels were cauterised but the ureter, renal artery and renal vein all needed to be harvested intact along with the kidney.

The surgery had begun as a laparoscopic procedure but once the kidney was detached Janet needed to remove it from Rosa's abdomen. She enlarged one of the incisions until it was the size of her fist and pulled the kidney free. It had taken a little over two hours before Janet was able to lift the left kidney out of Rosa's abdomen. It was major surgery and Rosa would need several days in hospital to recover.

In the second theatre, Rob's kidney was also being removed. It would be packed in ice and preservation fluid before being put in a medical tissue cool bag for collection by the courier company. They would take it to the airport and it would then head for Brisbane on the late morning flight.

Grace made a call to the courier company to confirm collection at the other end before checking the status of Rosa kidney. Elliot held her excised kidney in his gloved hands, checking Janet's handiwork. He looked up at Grace in the viewing gallery and, after returning Rosa's kidney to the iced water, he gave a thumbs-up signal to Grace, indicating that Rosa's kidney was looking good.

That kidney didn't have far to go. It was only going to a third theatre adjacent to the one they were in now to be transplanted into Paul. Despite their proximity, they still wouldn't meet even post-operatively. With private facilities there would be no need but if they wanted to communicate via letter Grace would assist them to do that. Often it was a useful exercise, for the donor in particular.

Even though living donors were usually donating a kidney to help out a loved one and therefore could see first-hand the difference a kidney transplant could make, they still often experienced feelings of loss. Hearing from the 'other half' in the exchange process, the person who received their gift of a kidney and the gift of a normal life could be immensely satisfying and help in their recovery process. They were often prepared for the financial losses incurred when they needed to take time off work, often weeks, to recover, but the emotional side of relinquishing a body part was often more stressful than they had anticipated.

Grace's role didn't end today. She would continue to liaise with and counsel all four of her patients. But having witnessed two successful harvesting procedures, she let herself relax just slightly as she slipped out of the viewing gallery to update Paul and arrange for him to be brought to Theatre.

He was in his room, ready and waiting in a hospital gown.

'How's it going? How's Rob?' he asked after his brother.

'He's doing well,' she told him. 'The surgeons are just closing him up now. All going to plan we'll have you in Recovery together in a few hours.'

'My kidney is already here?'

'It is and it's looking good.' Paul had never been told where his kidney was coming from and Grace knew it would be a relief to him to know that it was safely in the hospital. He didn't need to know it had literally come from across the hall. 'It's time to get you to Theatre,' she said.

All the other retrievals had gone to plan too. There had been no hiccups and apparently all the kidneys appeared viable. The courier process had begun and Grace's phone was never out of her hand as she kept tabs on all the transfers.

By midday Paul's surgery was under way, Rob's kidney was on its way to Brisbane, a third was on a flight from Brisbane down to Sydney, a fourth was being flown from Sydney to Melbourne and Rosa's son Steve was waiting in Melbourne for his kidney to be couriered across the city. It was enough to make her head spin but there was still one final piece in the puzzle. The one thing Grace was waiting for now was Connie's kidney, which was coming from Melbourne.

Her phone vibrated. Margie, the renal transplant co-ordinator in Melbourne, was on the line. 'Grace, the kidney is good. It's packed and on its way to the airport. I'll email you the courier tracking number.'

'Okay, thanks.' Grace checked the time on her phone as she disconnected the call. Five minutes past twelve. It was cutting it fine but she knew the airline was expecting the delivery.

She opened Margie's email and copied the tracking number into the courier's app and followed the progress of her delivery along Melbourne's freeways. She paced the hospital corridors as she constantly updated the app. Her stomach rumbled, making her realise how long ago breakfast had been. She pulled a protein bar from her pocket. She should probably go and get something more substantial for lunch but she didn't know if she could sit still long enough to eat anything. A bar on the run would have to suffice for now.

The tracking app showed the courier van had reached Tullamarine Airport at twelve forty-five. Her incoming mail notification flashed and a message popped up. The kidney had been delivered. Step two was complete. Now she needed to make sure it got put on the plane. She logged out of the courier company's app and opened the airline's web page to check the flight schedule. It showed the plane was still due to depart at one-fifteen and should land just after half past two. If everything went smoothly from here on, Connie should be in Theatre for a mid-afternoon surgery.

Grace updated Connie and the surgical team before checking on all the donor patients, who were now in various recovery suites around the country. So far, so good.

At one twenty the airline website marked the plane from Melbourne as 'Departed' but just as Grace was about to give another update to all concerned, the message changed and the plane was now listed as 'Delayed'. She frowned. How could it have taken off and now be 'delayed'?

She called the airline to check and was told the plane had left the terminal but hadn't taken off. It had a problem with its steering and had had to turn back. They were trying to fix it.

At two o'clock the website was still show-ing the flight as delayed and Grace was get-ting nervous. She placed another call and was given the same information—they were trying to fix the problem.

'Is there another flight you can put it on?' she asked.

'The next scheduled flight is at four, we're hoping to have the problem fixed by then.'

Grace hoped so too. She desperately wanted that kidney but it was completely out of her hands. Her heart was racing in her chest and she willed herself to stay calm. This was a big operation, her first major project as the renal transplant co-ordinator, and while she knew that, technically, it was out of her control she really didn't want anything to be screwed up. There was absolutely nothing she could do but she hated this feeling of powerlessness.

She should update everyone but she was reluctant to do that until she had more concrete information. At this stage everyone in Sydney would assume the kidney was on its way. She would update them when she had the facts to give them. She took a deep breath and sat down to wait.

Forty-five minutes later she knew she had to tell people something. They would be expecting to hear that the kidney had landed. She called the airline again and was told that the passengers and cargo were being unloaded and would be transferred to another flight when a plane became available.

'I need that kidney urgently,' Grace said, trying to quell the rising panic in her chest. 'Can you please get it on the next flight to Sydney, the one scheduled for four o'clock? It doesn't have to come with those passengers.'

'I will make sure of it,' the airline representative told her, but Grace's confidence was shaky.

She knew the kidney could stay on ice for hours but she was desperately worried that it would get misplaced or overlooked. She wanted it on a plane and then arriving safely in her hospital, but whatever happened she couldn't wait any longer to apprise people of the situation. She ended the call and headed for the PR department. They would be relatively easy to deal with. Then she'd tell Connie.

She took the news surprisingly well but Grace deliberately made it sound as though she had the situation under control. She left the surgical team until last. She'd start with Elliot.

As head of the team she should speak to him first but she had to walk past Marcus's office to reach Elliot. Marcus was the lead surgeon on Connie's transplant so should she speak to him now?

She hesitated outside his door, but realised she was more nervous about telling him than Elliot. She didn't want to be the one bearing bad news to Marcus. She could only imagine the reception she would get as he was cool towards her at the best of times. Maybe she should stick with her plan and tell Elliot first. She knew he would understand. She'd tell him first and then *he* could tell Marcus.

That was a good solution.

But as she turned away from Marcus's door she saw him rounding the corner and heading her way.

'Are you looking for me?' he asked as he kept walking towards her.

She was caught, stranded between a rock and a hard place. There was no way she could pretend she hadn't seen him. She bit the bullet. 'I have an update on the kidney,' she said.

'Has it arrived?'

Grace shook her head. 'Not yet.'

'Is there a problem?'

He seemed to be standing very close to her. Maybe it was just that he was so much taller than her, so much bigger. She didn't feel intimidated but she did feel very aware of him, aware of the breadth of his chest, the warmth of his body and the smell of his aftershave. He smelt of the beach, of salt water and fresh air.

How he could smell like that after several hours in the hospital she didn't know but she knew that if she closed her eyes she would immediately think of the ocean. She resisted the urge to close her eyes and answered him instead. 'A minor one,' she admitted, and hoped that was all it was.

'You can tell me about it in here,' he said as he reached past her and opened the door to his office. His sleeve brushed her shoulder and she could feel the warmth of his breath and the heat of his skin. His proximity set her heart racing but his gaze remained steely and cold. He was such a contradiction of sensations and he stirred feelings in her that she didn't want to think about. And she wasn't sure that following him into his office was a good idea. She hadn't been alone with him out of the public eye yet and his inscrutable façade made her nervous. But she couldn't think of a good reason not to follow him in. At least, not one that she could verbalise.

'You told me it was on its way,' he said as she stepped into his office. She had assumed he would blame her and his tone suggested that she was in his firing line. She could feel her temper rising but she knew she couldn't afford to lose her cool. Now was not the time. 'What's happened?' he continued. 'Was there a problem with the kidney?'

'There's no problem with the kidney but there is a problem with the plane.'

She breathed a sigh of relief as Marcus walked to his desk and sat down, putting some space between them. If she was going to have this conversation in here, with him, she need to be able to think clearly and she knew that would be difficult if he stood too close. If she could smell him, feel his heat, she wasn't sure she'd be able to string enough words together to make a sensible sentence.

'What sort of problem?'

'The steering. It hasn't been able to take off. The kidney is still in Melbourne.' Her sentences were short and stilted. She was still struggling to think straight, her brain apparently too busy processing other thoughts.

'I assume it's already on another flight?' His tone matched the coolness of his gaze.

'Not yet.'

'What do you mean, "not yet"? It's Melbourne to Sydney, there must be a dozen other flights it can come on.'

He sounded irritated now and Grace could feel her face burning. Did he think she was completely incompetent? None of this was her fault. But, as the transplant co-ordinator, she supposed the buck really did stop with her. It was her job to get the kidneys where they needed to go.

'The next one doesn't leave until four p.m.,' she explained, fighting to keep a neutral tone. Losing her cool with him was not going to improve the situation. 'The airline has assured me it will be on that one unless they can get a replacement aircraft that can depart sooner. I've explained the situation to Connie. She's doing okay. She understands and I've explained that the delay shouldn't affect the outcome of the transplant. The team in Melbourne was pleased with the kidney.'

'It doesn't matter how good the kidney is if it's not here,' he snapped. 'I want that kidney.'

'And you will get it.'

'Can you arrange to bring it with another airline?'

It had been a long and stressful day and it wasn't over yet, not by a long shot. Grace's nerves were stretched tight and her emotions were threatening to overwhelm her. She wanted things to go to plan and she hated the fact that there was a hiccup and she hated the fact that, because of the hiccup, Marcus thought her less than competent. She was close to tears but she wasn't about to let him see that his attitude was affecting her and she was teetering on the edge of a fight-or-flight response. Fight won. She had a redhead's temper, which she usually tried to keep under control, but something about Marcus pushed her buttons and she wasn't going to let him get the better of her. This wasn't about him and what he wanted, and she was getting annoyed.

She focused her energy on that emotion, which was more useful than feeling incapable, and, besides, she had considered all other possibilities and she didn't need him telling her how to do her job. She straightened her spine and tried to at least give the appearance that she was competent and in charge of the situation, even though they both knew that was far from the truth. 'The other airlines have a similar flight schedule,' she told him, 'and changing airlines means moving it from one side of the airport to the other. I don't want to risk it getting mislaid.'

'The longer Connie has to wait the more anxious she might become and you know that can affect surgery outcomes.'

He had a point but Grace would do her best to make sure Connie stayed calm. 'I'm not doing this on purpose.'

'I understand that but you have to agree this isn't ideal.'

It wasn't perfect but it also wasn't the worst thing that could happen under the circumstances. She wasn't sure why he was making such a big deal out of it. She was sure it would all be fine, why was he so pessimistic? 'Hasn't anything gone wrong for you before?' she asked.

Damn. The words had come out of her mouth before she could stop them. Stupid, thoughtless words. While she had no idea about the most recent twenty years of his life she knew his childhood had been far from perfect but it was too late now. She'd spoken without thinking and there was no taking back those words.

Should she apologise?

No. She knew that would only make matters worse. Apologising would reveal that she remembered more about him than he would want her to. She gathered he was a man who guarded his privacy zealously and she doubted he'd want to spend time reminiscing with her about his early years.

'Not lately,' he responded. His voice was deep and flat and his eyes were dark and intense. There was not a flicker of warmth in them. He looked at her like he was blaming her for everything that had gone wrong. Today and every day before it.

Grace felt her phone vibrate in her pocket. She broke eye contact to pull it out and check the screen.

'It's the airline,' she said without looking up as she took the incoming call and listened to the latest update.

'Your kidney is being put onto another plane,' the airline rep said.

'Have you double-checked that personally?' Grace asked. She didn't want to pass on false information. Not with the mood Marcus was in.

'I'm watching it being loaded now.'

Grace breathed a sigh of relief and was able to look Marcus in the eye again as she ended the call. 'They have a replacement plane. The kidney is being loaded now and is due to land in Sydney at five-fifteen p.m. I'll let you know as soon as it leaves the airport and is on its way here.'

'I'll be waiting,' he said, his tone dismissive. He nodded once, briefly, in acknowledgement, but offered no apology for his earlier brusqueness.

Grace took the hint and left his office. She had things to do now. Things that would keep her too busy to worry about Marcus and what he was thinking.

She called the courier company in Sydney to make sure they would be on hand to meet the plane and then went to let Connie know the state of play. She kept a close eye on the airline's website as well, not relaxing until she had seen the 'Departed' notation for her plane. Statistics showed that several hours on ice did not affect the success rate of a transplant but she wouldn't relax completely until the kidney was safely delivered to her.

This delay meant the journey was similar to transporting a kidney from Perth in Western Australia to the east coast. It wasn't ideal but it had happened before without problems. How long the kidney spent on ice was far less important than how good the kidney was and, by all reports, the team in Melbourne was very happy with it. Grace had to believe everything would be okay.

Marcus was ready. He took a calming breath, preparing himself for surgery, but he wasn't nervous or tense. He'd been preparing for this moment for days, years really if he considered all the study he'd done. He'd performed numerous transplants before but he'd never been involved in something on this scale. He was excited, filled with anticipation, and he couldn't wait to get started.

He looked around at his team. They were in for a late night. It was after six already and Connie's surgery would take several hours but the sense of excitement and anticipation was palpable in the theatre. Everyone was happy to be involved.

Connie had been prepped and had moved herself onto the operating table but Marcus hadn't given the go-ahead for her to be anaesthetised yet. He wanted to see the kidney first. There was no point knocking Connie out if he decided the kidney wasn't viable.

'The moment of truth,' he said as he removed the lid of the container and lifted the kidney from its icy bed in his gloved hands. It was a good size without being too large for Connie and it looked healthy. He inspected it carefully and then smiled behind his mask. 'We are good to go, people. Let's do this.'

He put the kidney back in its bath. It would be warmed up later, ready to transplant, and returned to the operating table. His heart skipped a beat as he caught a glimpse of Grace standing on the opposite side of the room, a little behind the surgical team. Even though she was dressed in the same shapeless blue scrubs that everyone else was wearing, her face hidden behind a mask and her fiery hair disguised under a cap, there was no mistaking her.

He hadn't anticipated that she'd be in the theatre and her presence made him feel unexpectedly nervous. And not just because she would be watching and possibly judging his skills. She made him feel nervous in other ways as well. The way his body reacted to her presence was unsettling. He knew he was too aware of her and that made him uncertain. He hated feeling out of control and that was *exactly* how she made him feel. But he had no good reason to ask her to leave. He had to ignore her and get on with his job.

He looked down at Connie. The anaesthetist had sedated her and she was now asleep, draped in sterile cloths, her abdomen exposed and washed with an antiseptic solution, ready for surgery. Marcus held his hand out. 'Scalpel.'

The weight of the scalpel was reassuring, reminding him that this was what he did. This was what he was good at. He was a surgeon, competent, skilled, precise. He might not be any good at relationships, at social pleasantries or thinking about the past, but he was an excellent surgeon.

He blocked out all thoughts of Grace and focused on his breathing, on slowing his heartbeat and steadying his hand ready to make the first incision. This was his chance to show her how far he'd come. To show her that he wasn't that adolescent from Toowoomba any more.

He placed the tip of the scalpel on Connie's skin and sliced through the soft flesh of her abdomen. The blade cut through the skin and subcutaneous fat just above her left pelvic bone. He breathed out steadily as he made the first cut. He was calm, focused and relaxed now that surgery had begun. This was where he was most comfortable. Circumstances had made him determined to escape, excel and succeed, and his skills as a surgeon were the culmination of his drive and years of hard work and dedication. For him, being in the operating theatre represented the pinnacle of his achievements and it was something he was immensely proud of. He was good at his job and he was in control.

He continued to cut through layers of tissue. Cut, cauterise and control until he was inside Connie's abdominal cavity. He made some space for the donor kidney. The donated organ was from the right-hand side of the donor but he would position it on Connie's left, below her existing kidneys, as that made it easier to connect the ureter to the bladder. Connie's old kidneys would remain in situ higher up in her abdomen, protected by her rib cage.

As he worked he imagined he could feel Grace watching him. What was she thinking? He knew he owed her an apology for his earlier behaviour. He'd been abrupt and discourteous and that didn't sit well with him. Nervousness had made him harsh. He hadn't been nervous about the surgery itself but about how he would appear to his team. It was important for him to be in control and for others to see him that way. Losing that donated kidney or losing control was something he couldn't risk. He would complete this surgery and then he would figure out how to apologise to Grace.

The donor kidney was ready, warmed and waiting. It was gently placed into position and Marcus could then begin the delicate task of connecting it to Connie. The renal artery and vein had been carefully preserved and with tiny, precise sutures he attached these vessels to the external iliac artery and vein, ready to bring the kidney back to life. Once he was satisfied, the vessels were unclamped and he watched the blood flow closely, checking for any signs of leakage at the suture lines.

All good. Step two was complete. Now he needed to move on to step three, to connect the ureter. This was a straightforward process. Access and visibility was good and his hand was steady. His confidence was high as he completed the surgery. Once the ureter was connected he inserted a catheter into Connie's bladder and gave a silent prayer of thanks when he saw fresh urine flow into the bag. Immediate urine output sometimes occurred when kidneys from living donors were transplanted and it was always a good sign. The kidney was healthy and functioning.

He did a final inspection of his handiwork before closing Connie's wound with small stitches. He could have used staples but he preferred stitches as they would leave a less obvious scar, which he felt was important in a female of Connie's age. He might not understand much about women but he knew the importance of appearance. Once he was confident that everything was working, he instructed the anaesthetist to reverse the anaesthetic and thanked and congratulated his team.

'Great work, everyone.'

Surgery had gone smoothly and he breathed out a sigh of relief. Once Connie was out of the anaesthetic and stable in Recovery he could go home. He could escape.

But it seemed Grace had other ideas.

'I think this calls for beer and pizzas at Billi's,' she said. 'You've all missed tea break and I'm sure you'd like a chance to wind down. Who's up for that? The hospital is paying.'

'Hell, yeah,' was the first response. Free food and beer was rarely declined, and this offer was swiftly followed by a chorus of positive answers with only a few declining the invitation. Marcus stayed silent.

'Dr Washington?' Grace queried.

He looked around the room before replying. It seemed the majority of the team was heading to the pub, barring a couple who had families, which left him no choice. He had no one to go home to, no family, no excuses. He nodded. 'Sure. That sounds good.'

In the time it had taken him to shower and dress and check on Connie's recovery, Marcus had changed his mind about stopping in at Billi's Bar at least a dozen times. Even as he walked into the bar he was still in two minds about whether or not this was a good idea. He didn't drink and he didn't socialise. These situations made him feel awkward and he did his best to avoid them. He was never one hundred per cent comfortable in a group setting. The trace of the uncertain boy remained, always making him wonder how people perceived him, what people thought of him and whether he was saying the right thing.

In a hospital and particularly in an operating theatre he knew how to behave. He'd taught himself those skills but he always felt like he failed dismally with any social interactions. He'd never had a foundation for that. The psychological scars of his childhood ran deep and not even his surgeon's confidence could hide them completely.

Even in Theatre tonight he'd taken a moment or two to reply to Grace's invitation because it had taken him a few seconds to work out what he was expected to do. He'd waited to take his cues from the others and when it had seemed the majority of the surgical team was going to the bar he'd found himself accepting the invitation. Because it had seemed to be expected. It was pushing him out of his comfort zone but declining the invitation would have drawn more attention to him so it had been safer to accept. He didn't want to examine whether he'd been more enticed to accept because Grace had organised it, because she would be there, but that was beside the point now. He was here. So he would use this opportunity to apologise to her and then he would leave.

She was the first person he looked for when he stepped through the door and the first person he saw. Even in the dark recesses of the bar her bright hair shone like a beacon.

He'd been totally aware of her in Theatre today and not solely because he remembered her from his childhood. Recollections of her were still vague and triggered mainly by the unusual colour of her hair, but he couldn't deny he felt some sort of connection to her. Somehow he'd managed to keep his focus on his work and he'd kept up the required amount of conversation with the theatre staff, but even though Grace had stayed silently in the background, he'd been totally aware of her presence. He'd wanted to do his best work, not only because he was the new kid on the block but because he'd wanted to impress her.

An unfamiliar twinge of desire unwound in his belly as he watched her profile now as she chatted animatedly with her workmates. She looked completely comfortable and vibrant and he found it difficult to keep his eyes off her. He didn't want to admit it but the connection he felt was attraction.

And that put him on the back foot. He was completely out of his depth emotionally and he knew that usually made him defensive so he'd have to watch himself. He'd come here to apologise, not to make matters worse.

He wanted Grace to like him, he'd decided it would be safer that way, and he knew he'd been unpleasant earlier in the day. He knew he'd made a less than favourable first impression on her, but he hoped it wasn't too late to remedy the situation.

He made his way to the bar while he tried to sort through his new-found dilemma. An apology to her was necessary but he wasn't going to do it in front of a crowd of colleagues. And he had to work out how to deal with the fact he was attracted to her. That hadn't been a page in his playbook for Sydney.

He leant on the bar, half turned away from the group he was supposed to be joining as he ordered a soft drink. He didn't know if he could force himself to approach his colleagues. Didn't know how long he would last, but his position at the bar enabled him to keep half an eye on Grace. He couldn't resist. She looked up and met his gaze. She gave him a half-smile, picked up a pizza box and started moving. Was she coming to him?

Marcus couldn't take his eyes off her as she crossed the room.

He wondered whether she had someone to go home to or whether she was single like him. Would she have organised pizzas for everyone if she had someone waiting at home for her? Probably. She seemed like that type of person—one who was good at looking after others.

He very much doubted she was single. Girls like her never were. She was vivacious, determined, opinionated and fiery. If she was single it was because she wanted to be, he thought as she stopped in front of him.

'Hungry?' she asked as she flipped the lid open to reveal a pepperoni pizza.

He was starving and the pizza smelt fantastic but he didn't think he could eat a thing. He felt like the adolescent schoolboy of years ago. A bundle of nerves and insecurities. Why did she make him feel so nervous? Was it because she was linked to his past? A past he'd rather forget? Or was it because of the feelings of desire she evoked in him and that he was finding difficult to ignore? If he could work out why, and how, she made him feel this way he'd be able to fix it. He'd be back in control, but for now he felt like making a run for it.

But he had come here with the intention of apologising and she looked like she was about to present him with the perfect opportunity. They were away from their colleagues so he would apologise and then he'd leave. He shook his head and she closed the box, trapping the smell of pepperoni, but now he could smell her. She smelt fresh and clean and he wondered what perfume she wore. She looked pure, young, innocent and honest, but he didn't know if she was any of those things so before he could get distracted by how she looked or smelt he launched into his apology.

'I wanted to ask you to forgive my earlier behaviour,' he said. She was looking at him with a slightly mischievous glint in her amber eyes and he could see the corners of her mouth twitching. Was she trying not to laugh? Was she going to laugh at him? Could he not even apologise properly?

He repeated his sentence in his head. God, he'd sounded so pompous and pretentious. That wasn't what he'd intended. He tried again, accompanying his second effort with what he hoped was a self-deprecating smile. 'I'm sorry about earlier, I was being an arse.'

Grace's face broke into a wide smile and suddenly his day, which in all honesty had gone pretty well, improved even further. Her smile was amazing. Warm, wide and white, it showcased perfect teeth and lit up her already beautiful face. He couldn't help but smile in return.

'Apology accepted,' she said as she put the pizza box down on the bar and climbed onto the stool beside him.

Her knee brushed against his thigh as she swivelled on her seat and turned to face him. His heart missed another beat and desire swelled in his belly and settled in his groin. Hell, he was in trouble. He needed to get a grip.

She was just a girl. No one special. Just a girl with creamy skin, wide amber eyes and glorious hair, but there was no need to behave as if he'd been locked in a monastery for a decade even if he couldn't remember the last time someone had made him feel like this. He recognised the feeling. He felt happy. Open to possibilities. Filled with hope and promise.

He was being ridiculous, he chided himself. Women didn't make him feel like this. He was responsible for his own happiness. Being in Theatre, catching a wave or riding his horse made him happy. Not sitting next to a pretty slip of a woman. Operating, surfing and riding, those were his safe environments, the places where he felt he could relax and be himself without fear of ridicule or judgement.

In a hospital, wearing his white coat or his operating scrubs as a shield, was the only time he felt confident in company. When people deferred to his knowledge but didn't expect idle conversation. Other people, women especially, usually only made him feel uncomfortable and emphasised his awkwardness. He got a kick out of being at work or being outdoors on his own. But women he tried to steer clear of.

It wasn't always easy to do as there always seemed to be a new one on his periphery. He knew he was considered a catch. He knew that people assumed he was wealthy because he was a surgeon and he also knew, without being vain or narcissistic, that he had grown into his physical features and was now described as good looking. He knew it was often his unusual genetic mix that intrigued women, but that usually made him cautious.

Were they genuinely interested in him or was he an experiment? He usually assumed the latter, which gave him licence to indulge in casual relationships, giving the women a taste of what they wanted in exchange for sating a thirst in himself before letting them go on their way. No harm, no foul, no commitment.

A night or two of physical company. Nothing serious. Never anything serious. He didn't need a serious relationship. He didn't need the angst or the complication. Didn't need the heartache. His affairs were brief. They were about fulfilling a need for sexual release without any emotional commitment.

He didn't romance the women. There were no candlelit dinners, no bouquets of flowers, no gifts of jewellery, nothing that could give the women the impression that their relationship was anything more than sexual. They might share a casual meal, a glass or two of wine but there was no sharing of dreams. He was a master at separating physical intimacy from emotional.

In short, he didn't date. His spare time was spent on his surfboard or out in the paddocks on his horse and there was no room for a woman in either of those scenarios. It had been a long time since someone had even caught his eye. And it wasn't just because of her fiery copper hair.

Not that it mattered. Grace wouldn't be interested in him. She knew where he'd come from. She'd known him before he was Dr Marcus Washington. She'd known him when he'd just been Marcus. The quiet, lonely, sad little boy.

'I am sorry,' he repeated, keen to make amends and still worried that she would think him an arrogant surgeon, a trait so often associated with his profession. He could be called a lot of things but he didn't want to think arrogant might be one of them. You didn't come from a childhood like his and grow up arrogant. 'I don't normally speak to people like that. I wanted to make a good impression here and if I didn't get that kidney I wouldn't get the chance. But that was my issue, not yours, and I apologise.'

'Who were you trying to impress?'

You. 'Everyone.'

But mostly you.

He kept that thought to himself, feeling he'd embarrassed himself enough for one day. 'Having an opportunity to be involved in this paired kidney exchange wasn't something I wanted to miss out on. I'm afraid I got a little bit caught up in it all. Congratulations, by the way, you did a fabulous job with co-ordinating everything.'

'You weren't too bad yourself,' she said, with another easy smile. She was poised and comfortable and he wished he had some of her confidence. 'We've come a long way from Toowoomba, haven't we?' she added, and his heart stopped in his chest.

He still hadn't admitted to her that he remembered those days but it looked like his tactic of ignoring the obvious wasn't going to work.

'Do you think I could ask you a favour?' he asked, still choosing not to comment on her statement per se, neither confirming nor denying her observation. 'I'd appreciate it if you don't mention that I'm from Toowoomba,' he went on when she nodded.

'Why not? What's wrong with Toowoomba?'

The defensive note in her voice grated on his conscience. 'Nothing,' he responded. Not from most people's perspective anyway, but he knew his view was definitely tainted. 'But my years in Toowoomba aren't relevant to my work.' They might be relevant to other aspects of his life but he wasn't prepared to discuss that with her. He didn't even want to think about it. 'That's another thing I should apologise for,' he said. 'I told you I didn't remember you but I do.'

'Why did you lie?' Her eyes were wide. Was he imagining the hurt he could see in their amber depths?

'You took me by surprise,' he said honestly. 'I wasn't expecting to see anyone I knew. Or who knew me. And I'd prefer not to be reminded of my life there. I thought that if I admitted that was where I came from you'd want to talk

about it and I do my best to ignore those years.'
He was happy to talk about work, anything in
his professional life was up for discussion, but
that didn't apply to his private life. That topic
of conversation was off limits.

'I understand.'

'Do you?'

Grace nodded her head and his eye was
drawn to the glossy shine of her copper hair
as the light bounced off it. 'In a fashion, and
don't worry, I'll respect your request.'

He wondered what she meant by 'in a fashion' but he was reluctant to prolong any discussion about the town where they had both
grown up. He had no idea if he could trust her
to keep her word but as there was precious little he could do about that he had to take her at
face value. 'Thank you.'

'Don't mention it.'

Marcus stood up. It was time to leave. He'd
managed to tie up all the loose ends. His apology had been given and accepted. His expla-
nations made and accepted. He could move on.
There was nothing more to gain by staying.
Nothing good would come of spending more

time with Grace. It would only serve to confuse his already addled brain even further.

'Are you going?'

He nodded. 'This isn't really my thing.'

'After-work drinks?' she asked. She swung her head and looked around the bar and Marcus was enveloped in her scent. It wasn't a perfume, he realised, it was her shampoo.

'Yes.' Or talking about his past to an attractive woman. To anyone really. It was time to go.

She was a danger to him and his equilibrium. She'd been in his peripheral vision all day. Her red hair a fiery distraction. He'd blocked her out during the surgery and kept his head bent over his patient but the minute he'd lifted his head as he'd wrapped up the surgery his eyes had been drawn to her again.

What was it about her?

There was a fascination there but he sensed it was dangerous.

He was attracted to her but he knew it was risky.

He was in danger of exposing himself, his past, all his secrets. People saw him now as someone successful, intelligent, powerful. They weren't to know that it had taken him years to achieve that. But Grace had known him before. She was the very last person he should be drawn to. She was high risk.

She was gorgeous and good at her job and people, both staff and patients, seemed to like her, but seeing her brought reminders of the shy, unloved, unwanted boy he had been when he'd lived in Toowoomba.

Only he couldn't help himself. His attraction to her presented him with a host of complications that he didn't want or need. His nerves were stretched tight whenever she was near. She was testing his resolve. She was dangerous.

And he needed to stay away from her.

CHAPTER FOUR

GRACE HAD BARELY set foot inside her flat on Thursday evening when she received a call summoning her back to work.

'I'll be there as quickly as possible,' she said as she pressed 'end' and immediately called for a cab. On her way to the hospital she phoned Marcus.

'Marcus Washington.'

He was the on-call specialist for the night and, despite the fact she knew he would answer, the sound of his voice rushed through her and set her nerves jingling.

'It's Grace.' Her voice sounded breathless to her ears but she didn't think he would notice.

'Is there a problem?'

He was obviously expecting a work call and assumed there would be a problem. She wondered what he'd say if she told him she was phoning to invite him to dinner.

But she knew what he'd say. Despite their truce they weren't in that place yet. Their relationship over the past ten days since the kidney exchange surgery and the night in Billi's Bar had improved but it had remained purely professional. He was less cool towards her, but still reserved.

'Is everything all right with Connie?'

Connie was recovering well after her surgery and Grace knew Marcus had plans to discharge her in the morning. She would have frequent check-ups, as would Rob, but both transplant patients, and the donor patients, had experienced smooth recovery phases to date.

'Connie is fine,' she told him, 'but one of our other patients on the transplant register has been brought into Emergency. Her husband is asking for me but I know they are about to call you next for a consult. Can you meet me in the ED? I'm in a cab, heading to the hospital now,' she explained, wanting him to know that she couldn't divulge any more details over the phone where the cab driver could hear.

Grace was first to the hospital and had got limited information about their patient by the time Marcus arrived. The smell of Chinese food accompanied him into the ED, disguising his familiar fresh ocean scent, and she saw a carrier bag holding takeaway containers hanging from his fingertips. The bags drew her eye to his thighs, encased in well-worn jeans and topped with a white polo shirt that drew her eye higher. The white fabric skimmed his chest and highlighted his skin tone. He was casually dressed but looked just as good as when he was wearing a suit or surgical scrubs.

'Did I catch you in the middle of dinner?' she asked, wondering if he'd asked for a doggy bag for his leftovers. It looked like a large amount of food.

'No. I was just collecting my order when you called and I didn't want it to go to waste. I figured the staff would be just as hungry,' he said as he deposited the bags on the triage desk and told the nurses, 'Go your hardest.'

Grace knew they wouldn't need to be asked twice and Marcus had just won himself a few more fans. He turned back to her after being thanked. 'Now, I'm all yours. What can you tell me?'

Grace looked away quickly, flustered at being told he was all hers, afraid her face would colour with its tell-tale flush. She turned and led Marcus into a side room but not before he'd lifted two of the containers and some chopsticks from a bag. He put the containers on the stainless-steel bench and removed the lids to reveal six steaming dumplings and a dipping sauce.

'Want one?' he asked as he picked up a dumpling with his chopsticks and dipped it in the sauce. Her eyes were drawn to his long, slender fingers, his prowess with the chopsticks rivalling his skill with the scalpel.

'What flavour are they?'

'Prawn.' He handed her a pair of chopsticks.

The dumplings did smell good and Marcus *looked* really good. It might not be a dinner invitation in the sense she hoped for but in the interests of maintaining their truce she thought it would only be polite to accept his offer.

'Thanks.' Her fingers brushed his as she took the offered chopsticks and her skin tingled and sighed as it came into contact with his.

Not that Marcus seemed to notice. 'Okay, tell me about this patient.'

Grace dipped her dumpling as she gathered her composure. 'Louise Edwards. Age thirty-eight. She has end-stage renal disease and type one diabetes. She has her dialysis here so I touch base with her once a week since she's on the transplant register, but she presented today with hypertension, vomiting and dehydration. It appears the dialysis isn't clearing enough of the toxins from her system. The registrar is with her now and she called for a renal consult.'

'She's only thirty-eight?'

Grace nodded. She bit into the dumpling but had difficulty swallowing it, not because it wasn't melt-in-the-mouth delicious but because her appetite waned as she thought about Louise.

'What else?' Marcus asked.

Grace looked up at him.

'Something is bothering you. What is it?' he said as he took another dumpling.

'I know I need to wait for you to review her but it's not looking great. She has a young family. Three kids. She needs a transplant soon, before it's too late.'

Marcus finished the dumpling and threw his chopsticks into the bin. 'Right, where is she?'

Grace took Marcus to the exam cubicle and introduced him to the ED registrar, Louise and her husband, Daniel. Grace left him to his assessment and waited outside. The cubicle was already crowded and there was no need for her to be there. She had no idea what Marcus would be able to do but she prayed for a miracle, just in case.

He was out within ten minutes.

'How is she?' Grace asked, but she really only needed to look at his expression to know the answer. *Not good.* Her heart fell.

'You were right. She needs a transplant urgently. I've got her on meds for hypertension and nausea. We're running a drip but she needs monitoring. I'll increase her priority on the transplant list and then all we can do is hope and pray and wait that we get a kidney in time,' he said as he headed for the triage desk. 'Give me a minute to increase her priority and to make sure we have a bed for her and then

I'm going back to the Chinese restaurant to get some more food—everything here's pretty much gone. Would you like to join me?'

His invitation took her by surprise. 'I don't know if I could eat anything.' She felt sick with worry over Louise.

'There's nothing you can do for Louise tonight,' he said, reading her mind.

The reality was there was nothing she could do for Louise at all and that didn't sit well with her. Her natural instinct was to help people. To make things better. But Marcus was right. She was powerless. She really didn't feel hungry but she didn't want to go home to an empty flat either, as Lola was also working. Keeping Marcus company would at least keep her mind occupied. 'You're right,' she replied with a nod. 'I will come with you.'

Grace entered the restaurant, which was tucked down a side lane behind Billi's Bar. As Marcus held the door she had to remind herself this was not a date. The restaurant was small but brightly lit and noisy. It wasn't intimate or romantic.

'If you could grab a table,' he said, 'I'll get us some food. Any preferences?'

Grace shook her head. She slid into a seat at the only vacant table in the back corner of the restaurant and watched as Marcus's order was taken quickly. She wondered how often he'd eaten here in the short time he'd been in Sydney. The staff obviously knew who he was.

'Daniel said living kidney donation wasn't an option in this case,' Marcus said as he put a bottle of water and two glasses on the table and sat down. 'Do you know why not?'

The table was tiny and his knees knocked Grace's as he sat in his chair. Her heart stuttered, missing a beat. She took a steadying breath. They were two colleagues sharing a quick meal, she told herself. Nothing more.

She nodded and gathered her thoughts. 'Daniel wasn't a match and Louise has no siblings. Her father died a few years back and her mother isn't well. Unless a friend is willing to give up a kidney, and is a match, we'll just have to wait and hope. Do you want me to speak to Daniel again tomorrow and ask about any friends or cousins he may not have already thought of?'

'I'm not sure that we even have the time to go down that path,' he said as their food was brought to their table. 'Let's see what tomorrow brings.'

The food smelled incredible. 'I think my appetite just returned,' Grace said as she helped herself to the chicken hotpot, pleased to have something to focus on other than Marcus's face, which was way too close across the small table, and his knees, which continued to bump against hers. 'I had no idea this place even existed.'

'How long have you lived here?' He glanced around at the crowded space and sounded surprised that she hadn't found this restaurant before.

'Five years.'

'You're staying here?' he asked. 'No plans to go back to Toowoomba?'

'Not at the moment. I like Sydney. And not everyone goes back, as you well know.' She smiled, hoping that would soften her words.

He gave a quirky half-smile that lifted one corner of his mouth but didn't reach his eyes. 'But I assume you still have family there.'

'Yes. Don't you?'

'No,' he replied as he spooned more food into his bowl.

Was he avoiding eye contact? She wasn't sure. He didn't seem edgy. He looked relaxed. In Theatre he looked in control, in Billi's Bar he had looked uncomfortable but here he looked calm. They were packed shoulder to shoulder with the other patrons but, despite the crowd, it was the most comfortable she had seen him. She wondered if it was because no one knew him. Most of the other diners were speaking Chinese. No one was interested in Marcus.

Except for her.

She wondered again where his father was but she was afraid she'd ruin the mood if she pried.

'What brought you to Sydney?' he asked, ending the silence that had stretched between them.

'My career.' She still loved saying that. She was proud of her achievements and her career was everything to her at the moment. Despite the fact that it wasn't the whole story, it was enough to divulge for now. 'My sister-in-law had a kidney transplant down here and I found the whole process fascinating so I applied for a job in the renal unit and I got it.'

'Your sister-in-law had a transplant?'

His dark eyes watched her intently and Grace lost her concentration for a moment before she eventually nodded. 'She had polycystic kidney disease. She's the reason I'm here.'

'How's she doing?'

'She's doing well. She's married to Lachlan and they're happy, planning on having a family.' She paused, curious to know if Marcus would ask after Lachlan or Hamish, but when he stayed silent she continued. 'Her transplant was five years ago, just before I moved here, and since then I've worked my way into the renal co-ordinator position. It's new, I've only had the role for six months but I love it. And I can't do this in Toowoomba so...' she shrugged '...here I am. I get home when I can.'

'Which is how often?'

'I don't know. A few times a year.' Other than her family there wasn't a lot for her in Toowoomba any more. Her new life was in Sydney. Her career. Her friends. 'I go back for birthdays, Christmas, weddings, that sort of thing.'

'Do you go to lots of weddings?'

'Not any more,' she admitted. 'My friends who stayed in Toowoomba tended to get married early and they're all having their second or third babies now. Or getting divorced.' It was hard to believe now that had almost been her life too. Sometimes she didn't recognise that part of herself any more. The girl who had thought she was happy to settle down at a young age was long gone. The world was so much bigger than Toowoomba.

'And you escaped?'

'Sort of.'

'Sort of?'

She'd been looking for an escape. She'd wanted to get away from a place where she had experienced so much distress. Merridy's transplant had opened her eyes to a whole world of other possibilities. After she had lost Johnny she'd been desperate to escape and start again, and she had jumped at the chance to move to the city. She had some understanding of Marcus's reluctance about small towns and their long memories. She still carried the memories of her loss but the passing of time had eased the pain and the guilt. Johnny was gone but it had been his choice to go. Her choice had been to move forward and, with time, the wounds had healed and now she was able to visit Toowoomba without being haunted by the tragedy she'd experienced. But tonight was not the night for that story.

'I was looking for a challenge,' she said. Something to take her mind off things. She'd needed a new start and fresh surroundings and she knew that moving to Sydney had been the right decision. She'd embraced city life, its challenges, the excitement, and she'd needed to be somewhere that helped push the memories aside, somewhere where people weren't constantly reminding her of what had happened. Naturally she still wanted to find true love but she knew now that Johnny hadn't been the right one for her. She was prepared to wait. She enjoyed her life in Sydney and her job. The rest would happen in time. She was sure of it.

'And have you found challenges?' Marcus asked, bringing her back to the present.

'I've found plenty,' she replied. One was sitting opposite her. She suspected her quest to find out more about him might be the biggest challenge she would face in the near future. And it was one she was prepared to take on.

But rather than pick up on her comment he was looking at his watch.

'Are you going back to the hospital?' she asked.

He nodded. 'I want to make a few more calls.'

Grace stood, taking her cue from him. 'Thank you for dinner, I'll remember this place.'

Marcus walked her to the taxi rank in front of Billi's Bar and waited until she was safely in a cab. Grace sat in the back with a smile on her face. He might take some work but she thought Marcus Washington could provide her with both a challenge and some excitement. She looked forward to it.

Grace liked it when she had time to watch the operations. It was a reward for all the time and effort she put into getting the process happening. She spent hours counselling, organising and liaising, and she enjoyed watching it all come together. She loved this part of her job—a successful, happy outcome for everyone. Except for the donor family, although she knew from experience that the knowledge that their loved one's death was helping others often helped in the healing process.

And she particularly enjoyed watching Marcus. He was a completely different person when he had a scalpel in his hand. He came alive and she found it fascinating to watch. He was an excellent surgeon and there was no hesitation when he was operating. He made good, quick, well-judged decisions, whereas in other circumstances he was far more deliberate; Marcus hesitated before answering and appeared cautious.

She'd noticed that he held himself back in social situations but in Theatre he joked and laughed with his team and Grace hadn't seen that side of him before. It was like a mask had been removed. He obviously felt comfortable in Theatre. He was confident, almost chatty, although he still didn't share anything personal. While everyone else was talking about their plans for the weekend Grace still didn't have any idea what Marcus was up to but he joined in with the general conversation.

The discussion turned to music people liked listening to—he liked country music—and their favourite food. Grace already knew he had a preference for Chinese and knowing she was privy to that information before anyone else gave her a little burst of satisfaction. When the topic changed to where they were all going on their next holidays she learned his favourite place was anywhere he could ride a horse or a wave but, in particular, Margaret River, three hours south of Perth in Western Australia.

By the end of the surgery she'd learnt far more about him than she'd known at the start but it really only served to reinforce that they had nothing in common. She liked pop rock, the Blue Mountains and Italian food was her go-to. She couldn't surf, although she did like the beach but needed to be careful in the sun. They had nothing in common other than spending their early years in Toowoomba and they were now both working in renal medicine. But both things were circumstantial. Their common ground certainly didn't bind them together.

* * *

It was late when Grace got out of Theatre but she went back to her office hoping that by some miracle a kidney had been found for Louise.

But today was apparently not the day for miracles.

She went to visit Louise anyway, to see how she was, and found her room bursting at the seams with Daniel and their children. The children often accompanied Louise to the hospital for her dialysis during school holidays and Grace had met them several times. The eldest girl was quite solemn and Grace suspected she'd had to shoulder some of the responsibilities at home and, even now, she had her little brother on her lap as they read his school reader. Grace wondered how she'd managed to get him to sit still. He was only six years old and usually full of energy.

The second daughter was usually far more verbose but today even she seemed quiet. It was highly likely that they were picking up on the tension and stress and worry that surrounded Louise but Grace wasn't able to ease their concerns.

As she left Louise and her family she saw Marcus at the nurses' station. He was still in his surgical scrubs and had his back to her but she knew the set of his shoulders, the shape of his head, the length of his legs. She didn't realise she'd spent so much time studying him that his physique was imprinted in her brain but, then again, it was a very impressive physique.

She went to him. 'Are you going to see Louise?'

He nodded. 'I take it we don't have a kidney yet?'

'No.'

He picked up Louise's file but before he could walk away Grace spoke again. 'You didn't mention in Theatre whether you have plans for the weekend.' She went on hurriedly, not wanting to give him an opportunity to interrupt before she'd finished. She half expected she knew what he would say but she wanted to extend the invitation anyway. 'Lachlan and his wife are in town and I'm having lunch with them tomorrow. If you're not busy you're welcome to join us.'

'Why?' Marcus still wasn't exactly cheerful

and approachable but she felt he was less wary of her. His eyes held a little more warmth but his tone remained guarded, almost suspicious.

She shrugged. 'I thought you might like it and I owe you a meal.'

'No, you don't. Thank you, but I'm busy to-morrow.'

She wondered what he was busy doing. He hadn't mentioned anything in Theatre when everyone else had discussed their plans for the weekend. For a moment she wondered if he wasn't busy at all but was just brushing her off. Had she misread the situation? Mistaken his openness in Theatre for a willingness to socialise? His eyes had gone blank again.

She cut her losses. She was grateful that their working relationship had improved but she knew when her company wasn't welcome. 'No problem. Another time, perhaps.'

Grace liked people to be happy and she knew she had a tendency to try to make that happen, even when she suspected it was an uphill battle. She'd failed before but she didn't let that stop her. She would continue to try to bring some positivity and happiness into people's lives and that would include Marcus. She felt that he, in particular, could use some happiness but he didn't seem to think it would come from her and she'd have to deal with that.

Marcus sat out the back on his surfboard, waiting for his turn to catch a wave. He'd got home late last night and he'd slept badly but he'd needed to burn off energy this morning and surfing was his only outlet while he was in Sydney. Surfing was relaxing and he needed that today. Surfing gave him the opportunity to be part of something without having to be involved. He could nod a greeting or comment on someone's ride but there was no expectation that he would have a conversation or have to reveal anything about himself. It was a solitary pursuit, which suited him just fine. The only problem was that it left him with too much time to think.

He'd spent last night the same way he'd already spent several other nights, tossing and turning. There were too many thoughts racing through his head and he blamed his return to the east coast. He was battling thoughts about his past. About his mother and father. About Grace.

He wasn't sure what to do about most of it. Doing nothing about Grace would be the sensible option but it wasn't the one he was tempted to take. Thursday night was a prime example of not taking the sensible option. He hadn't needed to invite her to dinner and it was completely out of character for him to invite a woman he didn't plan on sleeping with out at all, but he'd done it anyway and he'd enjoyed it. More than he wanted to admit. And he didn't want to think about what that meant.

As he waited for a wave he caught a glimpse of a redheaded girl walking along the beach. From this distance it was impossible to see who it was but before he could really process his actions, he had dropped in on another bloke's wave. He knew he'd annoyed the other surfer but he didn't care. He had an intense, over-whelming desire to know if the girl on the beach was Grace.

He grabbed his board and carried it out of the water, heading in the girl's direction, hoping he looked like he was walking with a purpose and not behaving like a stalker.

Not that it mattered.

She wasn't Grace.

Disappointment flooded through him but now he couldn't get the thought of her out of his head. Not that he'd been having much luck with that before either.

He remembered the look in her amber eyes when he'd asked her to eat with him. She'd been hesitant, unsure. Of him or his motives? He wasn't certain but he could hardly blame her. He wasn't even sure of his motives. He seemed to lose all sense of perspective when he was around her. He was still awkward but something about her made him feel safe.

He should feel anything *but* safe around her. She knew where he came from, she knew far too much about him, yet he trusted her when she said she would keep her own counsel, and the time they'd spent eating and talking had been the most enjoyable social interaction he'd had since moving to Sydney.

He loved being in Theatre but that was work and he usually avoided all social activities,

or as many as he could, but something about Grace drew him to her. She was easy company. Relaxed and happy, not to mention vivacious and chatty. What was the saying? *Opposites attract.* Whoever had coined that phrase must have had them in mind. There was nothing to say that she was attracted to him but that didn't stop him from wanting to find out. Only the idea that it could potentially be a complete disaster was stopping him. She was too close. Much too close. Yet he knew he was going to have trouble staying away.

And he still hadn't worked out why she had invited him to lunch. He had no desire to see Lachlan. He didn't want anything to do with his past and he couldn't see the point of having a meal with someone he hadn't seen for twenty years and probably would never see again. But the idea of lunch with Grace was surprisingly attractive and he knew that if the offer had been to have lunch just with her he might have been tempted to take her up on it. So much for keeping his distance. So instead he'd made an excuse that he was busy. He did have somewhere

else to be but it wasn't nearly as enticing as spending time with Grace.

He knew it was one way to get his mind off her. It wasn't a pleasant way, but it was guaranteed to work.

He stripped off his wetsuit, strapped his surfboard to the roof of his hired four-wheel drive and jumped into the driver's seat.

'How is he today?' Marcus asked the RN on duty in the nursing home as he walked down the corridor.

Karlie raised her eyebrows. 'Not his best day. He had one of the carers in tears this morning. He was having trouble with his buttons but he won't wear a T-shirt and he refused to let the carer help him get dressed. He's been a bit agitated.'

Marcus steeled himself. He had visited every day for the past fortnight. Ever since he'd arrived in Sydney. He could handle this visit. He *would* handle it.

He took a deep breath as he turned the door handle and stepped into the room.

'What do you want?'

His father was sitting in a chair by a window. The garden outside was well cared for with neat lawns, clipped hedges and the occasional garden seat and bird bath strategically placed. Not that his father would notice or care.

Marcus remembered his father as a big man. He'd certainly been both physically and emotionally intimidating. Marcus's facial features resembled his mother's side of the family but he had inherited his dad's muscular physique. But his father had shrunk. Wasted away from a lack of nutrition and exercise. He wasn't old, only in his mid-sixties, but he looked at least a decade older. His skin was grey, his hair was grey and his clothes were grey. It was sad and depressing but Marcus didn't want to feel any empathy. He didn't think his father had done anything to deserve it but it was difficult to reconcile the old man in the chair with his memory of his father. A father he had avoided for twenty years.

He hadn't expected to feel so guilty. He knew he had nothing to feel guilty about, he and his father didn't have anything even resembling a functional relationship, yet he still felt guilty. If he hadn't promised his aunt he'd visit he knew he would find plenty of reasons to stay away. Starting with the fact that his own father didn't recognise or even remember him. What was the point?

He knew the point was that he still had the hope of a twelve-year-old boy that his father would pay him some attention. Would choose to love him. But he'd soon realised his hopes were going to be cut down. He doubted his father had ever loved him.

'I thought you might like a visitor.'

'Why? Who are you?' His father was looking at him suspiciously. They'd had the identical conversation every day for two weeks and Marcus prepared himself for more of the same. He was an adult now, he could handle a few weeks of this while he was in Sydney. Twelve weeks of repeated conversations with no connection in exchange for the one thousand weeks that he'd stayed away.

It should make it easier that his father didn't recognise him. It should make it easier to keep his visit brief and then to walk away but it didn't stop the guilt.

'I'm your son.'

'I don't have a son. You look like a Yank. Are you a Yank?'

His father had fought in the final years of the Vietnam War and his mind had regressed back to that period of his life. He didn't seem to recall having a wife, a son, a life after his early twenties.

Marcus shook his head and repeated. 'I'm Marcus. I'm your son.'

Marcus knew he looked nothing like his father would expect his own son to look like. Not if he didn't remember his wife, Marcus's mother, and the fact that she was from Barbados. His father was so anti-American, anti-Asian, anti most things that Marcus was finding it increasingly hard to believe that he ever would have fallen in love with someone who wasn't a white Australian.

Marcus wiped his hand across his eyes. He didn't remember much about his mother but he'd remembered her smile. He was so sure she'd loved him yet she'd left when he was only six. And hadn't taken him with her. She'd left him behind with a father who may have loved him but who had loved his vices even more. Marcus's memories of his mother were fleeting and he often wasn't sure which ones were real and which he'd created himself. By contrast he had plenty of memories of his father but none of them were pleasant. They were all tainted by the detritus of his childhood.

What a total disaster his life had been.

Which begged the question: what the hell was he doing here?

He knew why. He wanted some answers. That was why he was here.

He knew he needed some closure. His career was going from strength to strength but personally he was struggling. He wasn't happy and he knew he needed some information about the past in order to be able to make sense of who he was and where he had come from. He was terrified that if he didn't get some closure he could find himself following his father into addiction just to forget about it all. Just to block out the stories that had multiplied in his head. He had no idea how many of his memories were based on fact or how many had simply grown out of his imagination over the years.

Why had his mother left? Why hadn't she taken him with her and why had his father chosen to drink himself into oblivion?

'I'm not a Yank,' he replied as he sat in the only other chair in the room and unzipped his backpack. He pulled out a bottle of beer and noticed how that immediately caught his father's attention. He went quiet and still as he waited to see what Marcus would do next.

Bringing in alcohol wasn't exactly against the rules but it wasn't actively encouraged and yet Marcus had learnt that one small bottle seemed to calm his father down. He guessed that was how the slippery slide into alcoholism started. Just one to take your troubles away, and that became two and then three. Until you ended up here. In a nursing home, battling alcoholic dementia and advanced liver disease.

It was a horrible combination. But from the perspective that distance and a medical degree gave him he knew his father didn't have long left and Marcus couldn't really see the point of depriving him of the one thing he still got enjoyment from.

He cracked open the bottle and his father sat

up a little straighter in the chair at the sound of the unmistakable pop. He handed the bottle to his father, who took a long drink.

He pulled out another bottle for himself. A non-alcoholic version. Somehow it didn't seem so bad if it looked like his father was sharing a drink with his son rather than drinking alone while a stranger sat by his side.

It didn't look like he would get any useful answers today. He'd share a beer and then be on his way, he decided as one of the catering staff brought in a tray holding his father's lunch. Marcus wondered where Grace was having lunch with her brother. He imagined it was somewhere a lot more pleasant than here. He imagined them sitting in the sunshine by the beach while he sat in a room watching a stranger eat a sandwich and rice pudding.

But regardless of his circumstances, or because of them, he knew he'd made the right decision in turning down her invitation. What could he possibly have in common with someone he hadn't seen since he was twelve and, to be honest, someone he hadn't had much in common with even then?

Grace's father was a doctor, her mother was a nurse. His father was an alcoholic and his mother had abandoned him. The childhood he imagined Grace and her brothers had had couldn't have been more different from his own reality. Visiting his father was enough of a trip down memory lane without adding lunch with virtual strangers into his day. He had no desire to reminisce about old times. He'd spent far too long trying to forget them.

But that didn't stop him from wishing he was anywhere but here.

CHAPTER FIVE

MARCUS WAS BACK at the beach early the next morning. He'd learnt years ago that surfing was an excellent stress reliever and while he was enjoying his work in Sydney he was finding many other aspects of this visit less than relaxing.

His father's condition was stressing him out more than anything. If he was going to manage to continue with daily visits, albeit short ones, he had to make time to hit the surf as well. While he was at work he was able to block out all extraneous thoughts and focus on his job but away from the hospital he was finding it difficult to escape the memories and guilt without the release of surfing.

But when he arrived at Manly the surf was flat. He hadn't thought to check the surf report. After another almost sleepless night he'd tossed his things in his car and headed for the beach, hoping for the best.

The only upside of the lack of surf was that the beach was almost deserted. He untied his board and dropped it into one of the local cafés where he'd discovered they were happy to mind surfers' personal possessions provided the surfers made a purchase. He might not be able to surf but a swim might clear his head and ease the tension.

He swam for thirty minutes, parallel to the coast, up and back, until his muscles were fatigued but his mind was clear. As he started to tire he bodysurfed on a small wave into the beach. He rose out of the water and scanned the shore as he shook his hands dry.

A redheaded woman was walking towards him. She wore a visor that shaded her face and she was too far away to see her clearly but the visor left her hair exposed and it was definitely red. Once again, like yesterday, he imagined the woman was Grace. Was it the same woman he'd seen yesterday?

She was wearing a pair of short denim shorts with a long-sleeved top. Her legs were amazing. Toned and slim. It wasn't the same woman. He would definitely have remembered her legs.

He stepped out of the water onto the hard sand and continued to watch. A red kelpie streaked across the beach towards her, a ball in its mouth. It was definitely a different woman. There had been no dog yesterday. He intended to wait until she drew nearer but his feet were already moving towards her.

She was still fifty metres from him but the closer she got the more vibrant her hair looked. The closer she got the more her hair began to resemble the fiery copper colour of Grace's.

She threw the ball for the dog and it bounced high, headed for Marcus. The dog raced along the beach in his direction.

He stretched out his hand and caught the ball just before the dog reached him. The dog ran in circles around his ankles, waiting for him to throw it again. He reached down and handed the ball to the dog but the animal dropped it at his feet, not wanting to give up his game. He threw the ball back towards the woman and kept walking, meeting her halfway. The dog beat him to her. It *was* her. The dog stood looking up at Grace eagerly, waiting for attention, and he felt a surprising affinity with the dog.

He dragged his eyes up from Grace's toes, away from her amazing legs and up to her face. She was tiny, barefoot and barely dressed. Her copper hair glowed in the sun and her eyes glittered. She was looking up at him and smiling. She looked gorgeous and happy to see him. He couldn't remember the last time someone had really looked that pleased to see him.

'Hello.'

'You have a dog,' he said. He loved dogs. He'd never had a pet. Not in Toowoomba and not in boarding school. He'd had working dogs, farm dogs, but not a pet.

'Reg isn't mine. He belongs to Lachlan and his wife. I'm just taking him for a walk to let them have a sleep in.'

'Would you like some company?'

'I'm just on my way home, actually.'

Disappointment surged through him. He'd been so sure she'd say yes.

'Can I buy you a coffee first?' he asked, hoping he'd be able to encourage her to stay.

He threw the ball for Reg, needing to avoid eye contact. He didn't want to appear desperate but he wasn't ready for more of his own company yet. He'd spent a lot of time on his own over the past two weeks and while he was normally content in his solitary ways he suddenly found the idea of sharing a coffee and some more conversation with Grace quite appealing. He tried, and failed, to tell himself it was because his conversations outside work had been mostly one-sided discussions between him and his father, which had been far from satisfactory, but he knew the appeal lay in Grace's company. Nothing else. He was drawn to her. She calmed his mind but stirred his body. Made him feel excited but relaxed at the same time. She was the human equivalent to surfing—the antidote to his stress. He'd never met anyone who had that effect on him before and it was captivating. Reg returned the ball and he threw it for him again as he waited for her answer.

Grace hesitated, gathering her thoughts. His sudden appearance had taken her by surprise and she had a dozen questions swirling through her mind. What was he doing here? Why was he inviting her for coffee? And how good did he look?

She was trying not to stare but it was difficult when his bare chest was at her eye level. His body was brown, smooth and muscular. Droplets of water glistened on his skin, making him shine in the early morning light. His arms were strong and he had swimmer's shoulders, broad and straight. His stomach was flat, save for the ridges of his abdominal muscles, and she wasn't quite sure where to look.

He picked up the ball, which Reg had dropped at their feet, and threw it. The muscles in his shoulder rippled and Grace forgot to answer. She was mesmerised.

'My shout,' he added, when she didn't reply.

'Your shout?' Her gaze travelled below his hips. He was wearing a pair of short, red swimming trunks and she was pretty sure he didn't have anywhere to hide his wallet. He didn't have room to hide much in those shorts, she thought, feeling herself start to blush.

'I've got some cash with my car keys,' he said as he started walking up the beach. Had he seen her checking him out and followed her train of thought? She assumed he had—she'd been less than surreptitious—but at least he'd only followed one train of thought.

'And where are they?'

'Are you always this suspicious?' he replied. 'I promise I have money and I also have honourable intentions.'

That was a pity, she thought as she followed him. She hadn't said yes yet but she was intrigued enough by the invitation that she knew she'd accept.

'The café up there…' he pointed towards a small café that faced the beach '…has lockers for hire and they're also minding my surfboard for me with the expectation that I'll at least buy a coffee before I leave. They'll be happy to sell me two.'

He keyed in the code for the locker as they reached the café and pulled out a shirt. He threw it on, hiding his chest and disappointing her again. He placed their order and led her to a seat at one of the outdoor tables with a view of the beach.

Grace was aware of the sideways glances of several other café patrons as she followed behind him. All women. All taking a second look at Marcus. He looked fit, toned, healthy and very, very masculine.

'How did your lunch go yesterday?' he asked as they sat.

Grace wondered if he was being polite or if he was really interested. 'You really want to know?'

'I would. I'd like to hear about someone else's day.'

He sounded as though he had the weight of the world on his shoulders. 'You sound like you've had a bad day already.'

'Today's been good so far. Yesterday afternoon was nothing fabulous.'

'What happened?'

'I'd rather talk about your afternoon.'

'Are we going to have a proper conversation,' she asked, 'or are you just going to sit and listen to me talk?' She could see the sorrow in his dark eyes and her heart ached as she imagined all the things that could have put that unhappiness there. Grace hated seeing other people hurting and her instinct was always to try and make things better. That's what she did. But with Marcus she had no idea where to start.

'I thought a woman would love that opportunity.'

He smiled at her as he spoke. It was the first time he'd smiled at her and it was as incredible as she'd imagined. She quite literally felt her heart skip a beat. She'd always thought that was a silly expression. Until now.

'Possibly,' she replied. She wanted to make him feel better and he'd asked her to talk. Maybe he just needed a distraction. Something to take his mind off whatever it was that was bothering him. She could manage that.

'Lunch was interesting,' she said, as the waitress brought their coffees and the toasted banana bread Marcus had ordered. 'My sister-in-law, Lachlan's wife, had a really intriguing idea. You might like it but you'll need to hear the background first. Let me know if I'm boring you. I think I told you that Merridy had a kidney transplant four years ago. She had PCKD and Lachlan donated one of his kidneys. That's what got me interested in the paired exchange programme and the renal unit, but I'm getting off track.'

She paused and sipped her coffee before continuing. 'Merridy has become a big advocate for organ donation. She is often interviewed by the local media and regularly visits schools and gives talks but she has a bigger plan. She and Lachlan are on the land, they work with cattle and run a feed lot in Toowoomba, and Merridy's latest idea to raise awareness about organ donation and also to raise funds is to organise a cattle drive. Her idea is to get people to sponsor cattle in the muster or pay to ride along and the funds raised will go towards putting dialysis machines into country hospitals and training nurses.'

'Does she think country people will pay to do something they probably already do for free?' Marcus asked.

'It's not country people she's aiming for. She wants to run it for city people.'

'She thinks enough people would go out to the country to take part?'

'She doesn't want to do it in the country. She wants to bring it to the city.'

'To the city?'

Grace nodded and broke off a piece of banana bread and popped it in her mouth. 'You know how popular television shows set in rural Australia are. Merridy thinks there are plenty of people who would love the chance to be involved in something like this. She thinks it has an element of romance to it and that city folk would get behind it. There are heaps of young girls in pony clubs who would love it and people could walk with the cattle if they can't ride. She thinks it's the sort of event that would get massive exposure in the media and I think she might be right.'

'Where does she want to hold it?'

'This is the really good part,' she said before pausing for effect. 'She wants to drive the cattle over the Harbour Bridge.'

'The Sydney Harbour Bridge? Seriously?' Marcus's eyes were wide now but Grace was pleased to see that the traces of sadness had been replaced by amazement. If the idea was enough to distract him she could only imagine how incredible it would be if they could bring Merridy's idea to fruition. She could only imagine how the muster could inspire and engage other people.

She nodded. 'Yep. Wouldn't that be fantastic?'

'Is it possible?'

'We have no idea. I said I'd look into it. What do you think?'

'I honestly don't know. It's certainly an interesting idea.'

'Now I just have to convince the hospital, the transplant foundation and the council to get on board.'

'You're going to do all that?'

'Yes. Merridy will engage with sponsors. She'll do all the social media and sort out the registration process but we have to get approval first and I'm hoping I've got enough contacts in Sydney to organise that side of things. Are you going to eat that?' Grace asked, eyeing the last piece of banana bread. Marcus shook his head and pushed the plate closer to her. 'You said you ride—would you support something like this?' she asked.

He didn't answer immediately and Grace steeled herself for a refusal before remembering that he was a man who seemed to consider his answers and organise his thoughts before verbalising them. He was measured and calm, quite the opposite of her. Her tendency was to speak first and think later.

'Yes,' he finally declared.

'Where did you learn to ride?'

'In Western Australia.'

'Is that where you went when you disappeared?'

His brow furrowed. 'I didn't disappear.'

Another prime example of her shooting her mouth off and then thinking afterwards, she realised. She shrugged. 'One minute you were living around the corner and the next you weren't. People wondered what had happened to you.'

Marcus hadn't thought anyone would have given him, or his circumstances, a minute's consideration after he'd left Toowoomba.

'Why would anyone wonder where I'd gone?'

Grace looked uncomfortable. She picked up her coffee and drank from the cup, even though he was sure she'd already finished it, avoiding direct eye contact.

'I don't know. You became a bit of a local legend.'

'What does that mean?'

'People wondered what had happened to you and when no one knew, I guess they came to their own conclusions.'

'What sort of conclusions?'

'They were just stories…' she said quickly.

'What sort of stories?'

'We were only kids. You know what they're like.'

Marcus knew all too well what kids were like. It was one reason why he'd been happy to leave Toowoomba and never return. 'What stories?' he repeated.

She hesitated before answering. Considering her reply, he assumed, but her reply when it came took him by surprise. 'The one that freaked me out the most was when they said you'd been murdered.'

'Murdered! By whom?'

'I don't know,' Grace said, but he knew she was being evasive. He wasn't going to force her to tell him, though.

'Nothing happened to me. I just went to boarding school.'

'In Western Australia?'

He nodded.

'Was your mother there?' she asked.

'No. Why would you think that?'

'You never came back. Who did you stay with? You can't have been at school all year.'

'I spent holidays with my aunt and uncle and cousins on their farm down near Margaret River.' He'd never wanted to return to Toowoomba, not then and not now. He'd left that behind a long time ago.

'What happened to your mother?'

'I have no idea. My aunt said she just packed up and left one day.'

'You've never heard from her since then?' Grace asked softly.

'No.'

'Have you tried to find her?'

He had but he'd been unable to find any trace of her. Eventually he'd figured she'd changed her name and simply didn't want to be found.

Grace was sitting, watching and waiting for an answer, her creamy skin, amber eyes, innocent expression and amazing hair casting a spell over him, tempting him to let his guard down. But he couldn't do that. Didn't do that. Ever. Things went awry whenever he was tempted to.

'I looked for her. Unsuccessfully,' he said, deciding that was enough information to reveal, reminding himself that Grace was the last person he should reveal anything to. She already knew too much about him.

But he couldn't deny she was easy company. He wouldn't go as far as to say he enjoyed it, he wasn't one to enjoy the company of others, he was a solitary man, but Grace was so open and engaging. It was an unfamiliar experience to share a meal with no expectations.

Normally his conversations with women were work-related or very limited. In a social setting it was only a means to an end and conversation was almost always instigated by the woman. Conversation usually consisted of an introduction, maybe they'd share a drink and talk about what they did for work and then they'd share a bed. A single night usually. There was no talk of anything private or personal. He made sure of that. And his relationships didn't last long enough to include walking a dog and sharing breakfast. He made sure of that too.

'I'm sorry,' Grace said as she reached out and put her hand over his. Her hand was cool and soft and small and her pale skin was a sharp contrast to the darker hue of his. He couldn't remember the last time someone had held his hand. Had they ever? He also couldn't remember the last time he'd been physically intimate with anyone. He didn't do intimate. Sex didn't count. Sex for him was a physical exchange, something primal and necessary, but it wasn't intimate.

He thought about withdrawing his hand but it felt good under hers. He thought about turning his hand over and threading his fingers through hers but wondered what she'd make of that.

He looked at Grace, wondering if he could read her thoughts in her amber eyes, wondering if she would give him any clues as to what he should do, but as their eyes met the waitress arrived to clear the table and his opportunity was gone. As if realising what she'd done, Grace looked at her hand, lifted it and removed it from his. Then she removed herself. She stood up and picked up Reg's lead. 'Thank you for the coffee. I'd better get Reg home before he starts a ruckus. He's not good at doing nothing.'

And before he could say anything she was gone. Leaving him alone again.

Alone had never felt quite so lonely before.

'We have a kidney!'

Grace felt like she'd uttered those words days ago. It had, in fact, been only hours since she'd received the phone call advising that a deceased donor had tested to be a match for Louise and Grace had set the wheels in motion. Marcus was operating now and Grace was sitting with Daniel, keeping him company. She longed to be in Theatre, watching Marcus work a miracle, but she knew Daniel needed her support. Waiting for news was almost as difficult as waiting for a kidney.

'Does it normally take this long?'

Daniel was edgy. Grace could understand that and he'd been asking a variation of the same question for the past hour, but now she was starting to wonder too. She should have had some news by now. The surgery had started well over two hours ago.

'Would you like me to go and get an update?' she asked.

'Can you?'

'Yes. Give me a minute.'

Grace headed to the theatres but instead of wasting precious time scrubbing in she went upstairs to the viewing gallery. It was late in the evening and the gallery was empty save for two interns. They were standing at the window and appeared tense.

She shivered as a chill of foreboding ran down her spine. 'What's going on?' she asked.

'Cardiac arrest.'

'What?'

The viewing gallery overlooked two theatres, maybe the interns were watching a different surgery, she thought as she hurried to the window. Her stomach fell as she saw that the second theatre was in darkness. They were talking about Louise.

Grace squeezed her eyes shut before opening them slowly, as if she might find that she was in the middle of a dream and that the nightmare would disappear if she blinked. But nothing had changed.

'What happened?'

'I'm not sure, but they've been working on her for over half an hour since the arrest.'

'Oh, no.' That was not good news.

She stood with her forehead resting on the glass. She held her breath as she watched but within minutes she saw Marcus strip off his gloves and glance at the clock and she knew he was calling time on Louise's life.

Poor Daniel.

Poor Marcus.

Those poor children.

The interns left the room as Grace stood still with tears rolling silently down her cheeks.

She pressed her hand to the window. Wanting Marcus to know she was there. Wondering if she should go to him.

This wasn't supposed to happen. No surgery was without its risks but no one would have anticipated this. Louise was supposed to get a new kidney and live a long and healthy life.

Grace sank onto a chair as she watched Marcus leave the theatre. She knew he would be going to speak to Daniel. She probably should go too but she couldn't make her legs work.

But she knew her dilemma was nothing compared to Marcus's. He had the unenviable task of telling Daniel that his wife was dead.

Her heart ached for all of them, Daniel, the children, Louise's widowed and now childless mother and Marcus.

She sat in the viewing gallery until her tears had stopped and she thought she might be able to stand. She went down the stairs on shaky legs, clinging to the handrail.

Walking out of the theatres, she saw Daniel in the Reflections Suite, talking to the chaplain. She didn't interrupt. She would get in touch with him later. He would be in shock and there was nothing she could say, or do, that would bring Louise back.

She went in search of Marcus instead, unable to leave without seeing him. She had to know he was okay.

Grace was told he was in the theatre change rooms. She waited outside.

And waited.

No one came out or went in.

If he was still in there he would be alone. She

knew this would have been a tough night for him. The toughest. He shouldn't be alone.

She pushed open the door and went in.

Marcus had no idea how long he'd been sitting in the change rooms. He was still in his scrubs, everyone else having long since left the hospital. He was cold and his spine was stiff. He needed a shower but his muscles felt as though they'd seized up and he knew it was going to be an effort to stand and make it to the showers. He didn't know if he could be bothered. He'd just sit for a little while longer.

Talking to Louise's husband had been a horrendous experience. How did you tell someone that their wife wasn't coming home? That your children wouldn't feel their mother's arms around them again, that she wouldn't be there to wipe their tears or kiss them goodnight or hold their babies one day?

Marcus knew all too well what it was like to grow up without a mother. He'd been exactly the same age as Louise's son was now when his mother had left him. The only difference was that Louise hadn't chosen to leave her little boy. He hoped the father held it together better than his had done.

He couldn't remember what he'd said but he'd never forget the blank look in Daniel's eyes as he'd processed the news and the sound of his anguish as the truth had hit home.

Marcus had no idea what sort of man Daniel was. How he would cope with his loss.

He sighed and dropped his head into his hands. He heard the door of the change rooms open but he didn't lift his head. He didn't want to see anyone, didn't want to make eye contact, didn't want to have a conversation.

'Are you okay?'

He knew the question was directed at him. The change rooms were empty save for him but even if there had been other people in there he knew the person was addressing him because the person was Grace.

But even Grace, with all her optimism and joie de vivre, wasn't going to be able to lift his spirits today.

He lifted his head from his hands. She was standing in front of him, a worried crease between her brows, her amber eyes unusually sombre.

'Not really,' he admitted.

How could he explain what he was feeling? The guilt, the grief. He knew it wasn't all about Louise. He had enough insight into his own mind to know he was dealing with a lot more than what had happened today but how could he tell Grace that? How narcissistic would that make him seem? How out of touch with reality? His thoughts were best kept to himself.

She sat down next to him. Right next to him. He could smell her shampoo. Light and floral. She smelt fresh.

Her leg pressed against his and he felt her warmth. She placed her hand on his thigh and he could feel the weight of her palm.

'Is there anything I can do?'

He looked at her pale hand where it rested on his leg. He almost believed he could feel the blood pumping through her body, keeping her alive. Warming him. He needed some of her warmth. He was still so cold. He turned his head to look at her. She was only inches away.

Her fiery copper tresses added to her vibrancy. Her hair was mesmerising. Looking at her was like looking into the flames of a fire. He wanted to reach out and wind his fingers through her hair. He wanted to reach out and touch her. He wanted to bask in her warmth. He wanted her to bring him back to life but he knew he'd only get burnt in the attempt.

He should tell her to leave him alone. Tell her to leave him to wallow in his guilt and misery and despair.

His normal routine in times of crisis would involve going surfing or taking his horse out for a ride but it was ten o'clock at night and his horse was thousands of miles away in Western Australia.

And Grace was right here.

He stared at her face. Her amber eyes had softened, her pupils wide and dark. She had a few bronze freckles scattered across the bridge of her nose and her lips were plump and pink. He could kiss her now and forget about everything for a few moments.

Was that the answer?

He knew it would take his mind off things.

He was sure that kissing her would be a hell of a distraction but would it be the right one?

He didn't know and he didn't care. Now that the idea had crossed his mind it was all he could think about and he didn't think he could resist her even though he knew he couldn't trust women. But one night of comfort couldn't hurt. What harm could there be in that?

He leant towards her. Her eyes widened and he could feel her breath on his cheek. Her lips were slightly parted and he could see the tip of her tongue, small and red behind her teeth. He heard her tiny intake of breath as he reached for her. He cupped his hand at the back of her neck, sliding his fingers through her glorious hair, and pulled her to him.

CHAPTER SIX

HE BENT HIS head and covered her lips with his. Her lips were soft and moist and she sighed as his mouth claimed hers. He'd thought she might push him away but instead he felt her lean into him. He could feel the curve of her breast, plump and ripe against his chest, and he felt the answering swell of excitement in his groin as his blood finally began flowing through his body again as Grace breathed life back into him.

He closed his eyes and increased his pressure. He felt her lips part further under his. Her mouth opened to his and his tongue explored her. She tasted of peppermint.

He wanted her closer. Needed her closer. He wanted to possess her. For her to possess him.

He lifted her easily off the bench and sat her astride his hips, her knees on either side of his thighs. He pulled her shirt from the waistband of her uniform trousers and slid his hand under the hem, resting against the warm, soft skin of her waist. He moved his hand around her back and undid her bra with a practised snap of his fingers. Her breasts sprang free and he held one in the palm of his hand as he ran his thumb over her nipple. A throaty moan escaped from her lips as she tipped her head back and broke their kiss.

She held onto his shoulders and arched her back as she thrust her hips towards him, closing the minuscule gap that had existed between their groins. His erection was thick and long between her thighs.

The fabric of his scrubs was thin but there was still too much between them. He wanted to feel her skin against his. He wanted her naked legs wrapped around him. He wanted to bury himself inside her. To lose himself in her warmth.

His hand stilled, his thumb resting over her peaked nipple. He could make love to her now but, while it might be the time, he didn't think it was the place. The hospital was quiet but the change rooms could be used by other staff at any moment. He needed to take this somewhere else but he knew he wouldn't be able to make it much further without tearing her clothes off or losing control. He needed to prove to himself he could stop. That he still had control. Even if it was only fleeting.

'I need a shower. Are you going to join me?'

Grace didn't stop to think. She was incapable of thinking. She was far too busy feeling. Her body was a quivering mass of nerve endings, her senses heightened, touch, taste and smell being flooded with information courtesy of Marcus's lips and fingers.

She nodded and this time she kissed him as she offered herself to him.

He stood and lifted her up effortlessly and carried her across the room. She wondered if he was afraid to put her down, afraid she might change her mind. There was no chance of that.

He stepped into the shower cubicle and spun around, holding her against him with one arm as he closed and locked the door. He pressed her back to the door, trapping her between his hips and thighs. She lifted her arms and he pulled her shirt over her head, disposing of her bra with the same movement.

Marcus ducked his head and took one breast in his mouth as Grace clung to him. His tongue flicked over her nipple, sending needles of desire shooting down to the junction between her thighs. It felt amazing but she wanted more. She was desperate for more.

'I don't think I can wait,' she said. She was barely able to find the breath to speak.

He set her down on the floor and she kicked off her shoes as her fingers tugged at the drawstring of his pants. She hooked her thumbs into the waist of his scrubs and pulled them off his hips, the palms of her hands skimming over his buttocks. They were tight and firm and warm under her fingers. She pulled him towards her, pressing her stomach against his erection. He stepped out of his shoes and scrub trousers in one go and reached his hand over his head and grabbed a fistful of his top, ripping it off over his head as she slid her pants off.

He was naked but, more importantly, so was she.

She pressed against him, her soft, pale skin against his warm brown muscles. She reached down and wrapped her hand around his shaft. It throbbed under her touch, springing to life, infused with blood. She could feel every beat of his heart repeated under her fingers.

His fingers slid inside her, rubbing the sensitive bud that nestled between her thighs. Her knees were shaking. 'I can't stand,' she panted. 'You'll have to hold me.'

Her eyelashes fluttered and her eyes closed as he lifted her up in one easy motion and she spread her thighs wider, eager to welcome him. She felt the tip of his erection nudge between her legs and held her breath as she waited for what came next but she felt him hesitate.

Her eyes sprang open as he said, 'I haven't got any protection.'

She had no idea if she could stop now. And she didn't want to. She blinked and said. 'I'm on the Pill. Are you clean?'

He nodded.

She took him at his word.

He took her at hers.

There would be time enough later to think about their level of trust and where it had come from.

'I want you inside me.'

She didn't need to ask him twice.

She wrapped her thighs around his waist as she spread her legs. She heard him sigh as he plunged into her. She enveloped him as he thrust into her warmth.

God, that felt good.

She moaned as he pushed deeper.

'I'm not hurting you?'

'No.' The word was a sigh, one syllable on a breath of air.

She closed her eyes as she rode him, bucking her hips against his, her back arched, and she was completely oblivious to everything except the feel of him inside her as she offered herself to him. His face was buried in her neck and she tipped her head back as he thrust into her, rapidly bringing them to their peak.

'Oh, God, Grace, that feels incredible.'

Hearing her name on his lips was her undoing. Her name had never sounded so sweet and she had never felt so desired. She gave herself up to him and as he exploded into her she joined him, quivering in his arms as she climaxed.

He kissed her forehead and her lips and held her close until she stopped shaking.

She had let him seek comfort in her body, had offered herself willingly to him, but, having experienced him once, she knew that once would never, *could* never, be enough.

'You look like you've had a good time.'

Grace hadn't expected Lola to still be up when she got home and she was surprised to find her in the kitchen when she bounced in with a broad smile on her face.

'I just had sex with Marcus,' she announced.

'You did *what*?'

Lola's reaction was just the one Grace had expected and she'd never imagined *not* telling her. It was a force of habit. They had shared a flat for the best part of two years and their friendship had grown to the point where they told each other everything and this news was way too exciting *not* to share. She started to fill her friend in on the details of the last part of her evening, all traces of tears almost wiped from her memory by the past hour, but she didn't get far before Lola interrupted her.

'You had sex in the doctor's change rooms? What if someone came in?'

'We didn't think it through,' Grace admitted.

'And how was it? Pretty good, by the look on your face.'

'It was amazing,' she said with a grin. 'He certainly knows what he's doing.'

Lola laughed. 'I suspect a man who looks like he does has had plenty of practice. What did he say to get you to sleep with him?'

'What did he *say*?'

Lola nodded. 'You always fall for the boy with the story. Someone who you think needs you in some way to help them fix their troubles. How did he talk you out of your clothes?'

She had a point. Grace's first serious boyfriend had died in tragic circumstances for which Grace still felt she was somewhat to blame. She hadn't been able to save Johnny and it had taken her a long time to recover from his death. And ever since she had been drawn to men who'd had some sort of crisis. Men who, she thought, needed her. Whether it was survivor's guilt or part of the healing process she wasn't sure. Sometimes the crises had been real, sometimes they had just been spinning her a story and she'd been caught up in the lies.

Most recently it had been Anthony, a radiologist who had told her a story about his wife leaving him and taking the kids. His heart had been broken and he needed Grace to help him recover. Only it had all been a lie. He'd still *had* a wife and kids. Grace knew she was far too honest and she expected the same of others, which meant she often didn't recognise the stories she was hearing were just stories. Not until it was too late.

But she was positive Marcus was different. There was something damaged about him, a deep hurt, and she'd known he'd genuinely needed her comfort. But had it been about her or had she just been convenient?

No, she didn't want to believe that.

'He didn't have a story,' she said. Not tonight. It hadn't been his story that had made her abandon her clothes, it had been the look in his eyes. He'd looked at her and she'd been able to see that he'd needed her to take his mind off his troubles. And she'd wanted to help. She hadn't been able to refuse him. He'd needed comfort and she had been prepared to offer it, had *wanted* to offer it. What was wrong with that?

But she wasn't about to admit that to Lola. Some secrets were meant to be kept. 'He didn't say anything. He just kissed me and that was it.'

'What do you mean, that was it?'

'I couldn't stop, I didn't *want* to stop.' There had been no subterfuge, no lies, no half-truths. She knew him. And she knew he'd needed her. But what she didn't know was what would happen next.

'What happens now?' Lola wanted to know, as if reading her mind.

'I have no idea.'

'This is serious. You don't do casual sex. It's always dinner and conversation, something that could be considered a date. Have you ever even had a one-night stand?'

'Who said anything about a one-night stand?'

'Did he make plans to see you again?'

'No.'

Lola raised an eyebrow.

'All right, I admit I got carried away,' she said, without sharing any further details. Lola would hear soon enough about the outcome of Louise's surgery and she didn't need to know how distraught Marcus had been. That was between him and herself. 'But I'm not sorry. You do this all the time, so why do you get a different set of rules?' She couldn't deny she really liked the idea of finding 'the one' but there was no reason she couldn't have some fun along the way. Lola seemed to manage that all right. She insisted she was happy being footloose and fancy-free. Maybe Grace should try it.

'That's not what I'm saying and I don't make the rules but you must admit this is out of character for you. What if that's it, one night, thank you very much, and he moves on to the next girl? I don't want you to get hurt. I'm not sure you're tough enough to handle it.'

Grace knew she wouldn't be okay if Marcus did do that to her, but it was too late to worry about that now. They hadn't made plans or promises. It had just been great sex and she'd have to handle it if he didn't want to see her again.

'It's fine, Lola. It was just sex.'

'That's not how you do things, Grace.' Lola's voice held a hint of warning and Grace knew she was worried as well as right. Grace had never had a casual fling before. She'd never jumped into bed with a guy on the first date, let alone *without* a first date. But while she heard her friend's concern she chose to ignore it.

'It's fine,' she repeated.

Grace lay in Marcus's bed, satisfied and also a little bit smug. Despite Lola's warnings she *had* seen Marcus again and this was the third time in a week they'd spent the evening together. He'd taken her to dinner at the Chinese restaurant again; it wasn't fancy but Grace didn't care, in her mind it was now 'their' restaurant and she was more than happy to eat there. With him.

And tonight, instead of putting her in a taxi and sending her home, he'd taken her to his apartment and now she lay in his bed with her knee nestled between his thighs, her head on his shoulder as she listened to him breathe. He had his fingers in her hair, playing with the ends, and she could tell his thoughts were drifting.

She longed to know what he thought about. They spent a lot of time talking about her. They spoke about work and her family, the muster and her friends. He'd shared a few stories about his life in Perth but he was reluctant to share more than that and every time she tried to change the topic he quickly changed it back, which made it difficult to get a sense of who he was. She did know he'd gone to a boys' boarding school from the age of twelve and had spent holidays on a farm with his three male cousins so it wasn't surprising he wasn't a good communicator. But she could teach him. It wasn't healthy to keep every emotion bottled up. She hoped he'd eventually learn to share his thoughts and feelings with her. Maybe he would learn by example.

She'd ignored Lola's warnings about getting involved with someone who wasn't planning to stay in Sydney and who was also emotionally distant. Was she setting herself up for heart-ache, as Lola predicted?

She'd decided she didn't care. Lying in his arms, she thought it was a risk worth taking. An opportunity she found she couldn't resist. It might end in tears but she couldn't walk away. He was sexy and smart and knew what he was doing in the bedroom—it was no sacrifice on her part. Besides, she felt he needed a connection to someone and, at the moment, she didn't mind that for a few nights or weeks it might be her. A few weeks wasn't long enough to risk everything. It wasn't long enough for him to break her heart.

'Are you going to Louise's funeral tomorrow?' he asked.

That was where his thoughts had gone. The coroner's inquest had absolved him of any blame but she knew he still felt a sense of responsibility for Louise's death.

'Are you?' she asked. She'd be surprised if he attended.

'No. I don't think it would be appropriate.' His chest rose and fell with his words.

Grace hated funerals but she felt a duty to attend. She sighed. 'I have to go.'

'You don't have to.'

'I've known Louise and her family for three years. I've seen her at least once a week every week during that time, so I think I should be there to pay my respects to Daniel and their children,' she explained. Louise's death was affecting everyone in the renal unit and Grace knew she wouldn't be there alone. There would be a lot of support for Louise's family, friends and the hospital staff who had worked so closely with her.

'I wish I didn't have to go. I hate funerals, they are so sad, so final. People talk about funerals being a chance to celebrate life but what is there to celebrate when a life has been cut so short? Louise should have been able to celebrate being alive. All those dreams shattered.' Louise had had everything to live for but now she was gone. Grace hated to think about all the things Louise was going to miss out on and all the things her children would miss too.

'Life isn't always like that,' he said. 'You don't always get to live happily ever after.'

Grace wondered if this was an opportunity for her to talk to Marcus about his childhood, he certainly hadn't had a happy start to his life, but before she could formulate a question that didn't sound too intrusive he had already shifted the focus onto her. 'This is about more than just Louise, isn't it?'

'Why do you say that?'

'In the work we do we lose people and we work out ways to deal with it. I know there are some patients we form stronger bonds with than others but Louise's death seems more personal to you than I would have expected. I'm not saying you shouldn't be upset by it but are you sure there's not more going on in your head? Who are you thinking about? Who did you lose too young?'

For someone who kept his emotions close to his chest he was quite intuitive when it came to other people. Grace thought about brushing his question aside—after all, that was what he would do to her—but she was too honest. And maybe, if she shared something important with him, he might learn to do the same with her. 'I lost a friend. A good friend,' she said, 'when we were twenty-two. It was too young and, even now, I still feel like there was more I could have done, *should* have done, to help him.'

'Do you want to tell me what happened?'

In the hours they had spent together Grace had learned that Marcus was a good listener. It was probably because he preferred to listen rather than talk, but she was prepared to talk about Johnny. She'd found it was better to express her emotions. That was something losing Johnny had taught her.

'Johnny was my first serious boyfriend. He was from Toowoomba. We met when we were still at school. He suffered from depression and it got worse as he got older. He was on medication but he hated the way it made him feel. Said the tablets dulled him, made him feel like he was existing but not living. It was an ongoing battle to get him to keep taking them. One day he stopped and I didn't notice. I was studying and working, I was too busy. Johnny had grown up in the country on a property where everyone had a gun. He took one out one day and shot himself. He left a note saying it was all too difficult, that living with the disease was too hard. He killed himself and I couldn't save him. I've hated funerals ever since I went to his.'

Grace had grown accustomed to Johnny's absence but talking about him still made her feel sad. Fat tears were rolling down her cheeks. Marcus wiped them away with his thumb. 'Do you still miss him?'

'I miss the friendship we had,' she admitted. 'We'd been friends for ever, before we started dating, and that's the part I miss. I'm not sure that I miss the future we would have had, and part of me is relieved that I got a chance to do something different from what we'd planned, but then I feel guilty about thinking like that.'

'Relieved?'

'Everyone assumed we'd get married, settle down to a life in Toowoomba, but I honestly don't know if that life would have been enough for me. I think I would have had a lot of regrets. After Johnny died I felt trapped by the emotion. There were too many people feeling sorry for me without knowing how I was really feeling. It was a mixture of grief and relief and that made me feel like a bad person. I had to get out of there, away from all the expectations and the sorrow. When Merridy came to Sydney for her surgery I saw my chance for a new beginning. I could start fresh, somewhere no one knew me. Or Johnny.'

'And yet...' she still lay with her head on his chest but she could hear a trace of a smile in his voice '...on my first day at Kirribilli General you were defending the small-town lifestyle.'

'Lifestyle maybe, but I never said the people were easy. Moving here was a good decision for me. I can go back now with a bit of perspective. I'm not the same person I was, I'm stronger and I've learnt a lot about myself. If I'd settled down five years ago I would have regretted all the things I never got to do. I know I need more challenges than I would have got in Toowoomba. I'm happy here. I'm happy, full stop.'

She still dreamed of settling down. She still wanted a husband and kids one day but she could wait. She wasn't prepared to settle for second best. She needed excitement and challenges and she suspected Marcus might give some of that to her.

'So that's the full story of how I ended up here,' she said as she ran her hand down Marcus's bare chest, 'and now I think that's enough time spent talking about my past. I, for one, have better things to do tonight.'

'Tania?' Grace approached the nurse at the nurses' station and introduced herself after reading her name badge. 'I'm Grace Gibson, the renal transplant co-ordinator. Someone called asking me to review a file for a patient who might need a transplant?'

'That was me. We have a patient who was admitted yesterday with end-stage liver disease and the specialist is advocating for him to be placed on the transplant register but our liver transplant co-ordinator is on leave and I need to know what the process is.'

'I don't have control over who goes on the register,' Grace explained.

'I know but the patient has a complicated medical history and I doubt he's suitable for a transplant. Would you mind taking a look at his file and just giving me your thoughts? It might help us clarify what to do next.' Tania retrieved the patient's case notes when Grace nodded and handed them to her as she elaborated further. 'He has dementia and is also an alcoholic. Not a reformed alcoholic either.'

The name on the front of the file caught Grace's eye: *William Washington.*

Was that a coincidence? She was certain that was Marcus's father's name but surely he would have said something if his father had been admitted to hospital?

She took the file to a vacant workstation and flicked to the personal details.

Age—67
Next of kin—Marcus Washington, son.

She continued to turn the pages, trying to get a picture of the man who was Marcus's father.

His address was listed as a veterans' affairs nursing home in the northern suburbs of Sydney. Grace did the maths—he must have served in the Vietnam War. Was that relevant at all?

She continued to flick through the notes. He was underweight for his height and blood-test results were less than ideal, with several relevant increased markers consistent with cirrhosis. Iron levels and platelets were also low.

From his notes it was apparent that due to social factors, lifestyle choices and his medical history he wasn't a suitable transplant candidate but Grace couldn't forget that Marcus hadn't said anything. She returned to the nurses' station.

'Tania, it says here his son is his next of kin. Do you know if he has been in to see him?'

Tania nodded. 'He was here last night when Bill was admitted.'

So Marcus did know and had chosen not to share that information with her.

Grace's job was to look at his file but she couldn't resist going to his room. She got to his room at the same time as the catering staff were delivering lunch trays. Grace offered to take his in with her. She pushed the door open and found Marcus's father lying in the bed, his eyes closed. He looked a lot older than the sixty-seven years she knew him to be. He was a tall man who was much too thin. His skin was grey and he looked shrunken.

'Mr Washington?' Grace said as she balanced

the tray against her waist and knocked on the door she'd just opened and stepped further into the room. 'I have your lunch.'

He opened his eyes and stared vacantly at her.

'Do you know where you are?' she asked as he continued to stare vaguely. 'You're in hospital. You were brought in last night. Are you hungry?' She put the tray on the overway table and pushed it over his bed. He lifted the insulating cover with shaky hands and Grace wondered when his last drink had been.

She stayed with him for a few minutes, making sure he could feed himself and trying vainly to make conversation. He either wasn't interested in talking to her or wasn't able to maintain a conversation so she eventually gave up and left the room. She had another member of his family she urgently needed to talk to.

She found Marcus in his office. She knocked on his door and entered when he looked up. 'I need to talk to you about a patient,' she said.

'Sure. Who is it?'

'William Washington.'

She waited to see how he would respond but he gave her nothing.

'Why didn't you tell me he had been admitted here last night?' she asked.

Marcus frowned. 'Why would I? It's not relevant to anything. How did you know he was here?'

'I was asked to see him.'

'What for?'

'His specialist wants to put him on the national register for a liver transplant. I was asked to review his file because the liver transplant co-ordinator is on annual leave and the nursing staff wanted an opinion from someone on the transplant team.'

'He's not a candidate for a liver transplant.'

'I know,' she agreed. 'I need you to talk to his specialist. Explain the situation.'

'I know as much as you do.'

'Marcus, I haven't seen your father in close to ten years. How could I possibly know as much as you about his condition?'

'Until I arrived in Sydney four weeks ago I hadn't seen him for *twenty* years. You're probably more qualified than I am to have the necessary conversations.'

'Twenty years? You haven't seen him at all?'

'No.'

She desperately wanted to know what had happened but getting any information from Marcus was like getting blood out of a stone. He gave her tiny snippets of information but the rest she had to go hunting for. 'Is that why you came to Sydney?'

'No. I came to Sydney for this career opportunity but I figured I could use this trip to see Bill before it was too late.'

'Too late for what?' she asked.

'For answers.' He sighed. 'Bill sent me to boarding school in Perth and my aunt became my guardian. Until this past month the last time I saw him was when I was twelve years old. He sent me off to the other side of the country with no explanation. We were never close and I can't deny I was happy to go, but as I've got older I've started wondering about the circumstances that led me to Perth. What was the catalyst?'

For once Grace felt like she could actually understand what Marcus *wasn't* telling her and it gave her far more insight into his character than she imagined he realised. He'd been hurt.

Not by a lover—but by his parents. Grace noticed that he didn't even refer to his father by that title but called him 'Bill'.

'You've been by yourself since you were twelve?'

'I spent school holidays with my aunt and my cousins but I learnt to become self-sufficient.'

He wasn't going to trust easily. She would have to build that trust. 'How are things going now with your father?'

'It's a complete waste of time. He has no idea who I am.'

'He doesn't recognise you at all?' That didn't surprise her. If the two of them had had no contact for twenty years it wasn't all that surprising given Bill's dementia.

'It's more than that,' Marcus said. 'He doesn't even seem to remember that he has a son at all.'

'Maybe given some time he will remember you,' she said.

'We both know he doesn't have that long,' he said. He clicked the mouse and woke his computer monitor as he dismissed her by adding, 'If that's all you wanted to discuss, I have work to do.'

Grace was ready to go. She found the whole situation terribly sad, loss of any kind affected her deeply, and she wanted to get out of there before she burst into tears. She knew he'd hate to see her crying for him, knew he would hate her pity, but she couldn't imagine how it must feel to have a parent who didn't remember you. But what was almost worse was the realisation that Marcus had been on his own for twenty years. No mother. No father. No siblings. He'd had no one to kiss him goodnight, no one to listen to his dreams, to tell him he could do anything. No one to love him. He had no one. It wasn't surprising then that he found it hard to share his feelings.

She headed to the ICU in search of Lola, as she badly needed to debrief, but by the time she found her she was in floods of tears.

'What's wrong?'

'Marcus—'

'I *knew* he would break your heart,' Lola interrupted as she wrapped Grace in a hug. 'What's happened?'

'No.' Grace shook her head as she sobbed into Lola's shoulder. 'My heart is breaking but not because of anything Marcus has done. It's breaking *for* him.'

Lola stepped back, releasing Grace from her embrace but not letting go of her completely. 'What does that mean?'

'He's all alone. His mother left him when he was very young and his father has dementia and doesn't remember him. Marcus has no one, he's been by himself for twenty years.'

'He's probably quite used to being alone, then,' Lola said matter-of-factly. 'Has he said he's unhappy? He seems fine.'

'On the surface maybe, but how could he be happy to be so alone?' Grace relied heavily on her family for support. She knew she would never have recovered from Johnny's death without their help, and even though they hadn't necessarily agreed with her move to Sydney they had supported her in that too. They had always been there for her and she couldn't understand how Marcus, or anyone else, could be perfectly happy alone. No one should be alone. She believed in love and family but listening to Marcus talk about his family she knew he didn't believe in either of those things.

'Grace...' Lola's voice held a hint of warning '...don't assume he needs help or that things need fixing. You can't solve all the world's problems.'

She knew that and she didn't want to fix everyone's problems. Just Marcus's.

CHAPTER SEVEN

MARCUS HESITATED AT his father's door. The visits weren't getting any easier but he had an obligation and so he continued to come, even though he wasn't getting any further in his quest for answers.

He knew Grace thought he should be more direct with Bill—she'd told him as much, told him he should ask specific questions if he wanted specific answers. He knew that waiting for Bill to volunteer information was never going to work so why couldn't he ask a straight question? Was he afraid of the answers? Afraid of the truth? Or afraid he wouldn't *get* the truth?

He knew Grace disapproved of his methods and he didn't want the stress of her disapproval on top of everything else. He didn't want to deal with any additional guilt. It was clear she would never understand the issues he and his father faced and she obviously still expected their differences to be resolved. But reconciling their differences had never been his goal and he had made his peace with that. Striving for that outcome was only ever going to end in disappointment but he'd hoped to get some closure, or at least some answers, but, because of Bill's condition, that wasn't likely to happen either.

He took a deep breath at Bill's door as he mentally prepared himself to enter and hoped Grace was there to act as a buffer. Her presence was the only thing that made the visits manageable. Her presence in his father's hospital room over the last week had eased the tension between the two men.

Grace had formed a connection with his father and Bill seemed to enjoy her company. With Grace there was no pressure, no expectation that he would remember her or anything they talked about. Quite literally, she just gave him company.

Marcus, however, remembered everything he talked about with her. He also remembered every minute they had spent together. Every curve of her body, every freckle on her shoulders, the feel of her skin under his hand, the smell of her shampoo and the way her dark eyelashes rested on her pale cheeks when she closed her eyes as he kissed her. He'd learnt a lot about her in the time they had spent together. That didn't concern him as he enjoyed her company, in bed and out, but he was worried that she was learning more about him than he wanted to reveal. He knew she wanted him to open up to her, but he found that difficult. He'd taken her to dinner, which, while not completely out of character, he always did before he had sex with a woman, not afterwards. *Never* afterwards. And he had never let a woman stay overnight, he'd never even invited one to his house before. He'd done things with Grace that he'd never done with anyone. He hoped he wasn't making a mistake.

She fascinated him and he wanted to know everything about her. He wouldn't normally bother to learn about the women he took to bed—did that make him selfish? He didn't think so as those women didn't care about him either. But he was beginning to care about Grace. She was kind and gentle and honest and he enjoyed her company very much.

He refused to be concerned about that. He wasn't here for long so he could enjoy her company for a few more weeks and then return to Perth, heart and soul intact. Secrets safe.

He was fully aware that he was avoiding the major issues in his life—his feelings about his father and his feelings about Grace—but he'd never let himself examine his feelings before and he had no idea where to start or even if he *wanted* to start. He was terrified of how exposed he would be.

The irony of the fact that he could cope with just about anything professionally and then become a mass of indecision and uncertainty around his father, who didn't even know who he was, hadn't escaped him. He just didn't know what to do about it.

He opened the door and stepped inside.

Grace was there and she greeted him with a smile. He knew she was trying to make things easier for him. She was trying to help him mend the bridges and he appreciated it but she didn't realise that the bridges had been damaged so badly a long time ago and there wasn't going to be the time or opportunity to mend them. He wasn't even sure if he wanted to, he really only wanted answers, but he knew Grace wouldn't understand that. She believed in happily ever after.

He didn't want to disappoint her but she wasn't going to get what she wanted as far as he and his father were concerned. He had the potential to forgive Bill, and it was obvious that Grace would like him to, but he didn't think he had it in him. His hurt was still raw after all these years. Grace would be disappointed in him but he felt incapable of doing anything else.

'Hi.' She was still smiling as she greeted him. 'I was just telling Bill about the muster.'

He'd noticed she always carefully avoided saying 'your dad' in front of him and Bill. The phrase agitated Bill and irritated Marcus. He appreciated her candour even though he couldn't be the son Grace wanted him to be, just like Bill couldn't be the father she wanted for *him*.

It was what it was.

He tried not to feel jealous that Grace had developed a good rapport with his father. She never seemed to run out of conversation. Perhaps it was because she was happy to chat about anything that captured Bill's interest. It was easy to hold a conversation when you weren't emotionally invested. It didn't matter to Grace what the topic was, her only agenda was to keep Bill company.

Marcus wished he could say the same for himself but he was too aware that time was running out. He didn't have months at his disposal to get the answers he was seeking. He didn't even have weeks. His father was getting frailer and it was clear he wouldn't be leaving the hospital to return to the nursing home. The hospital was his last stop. There could be worse things than having Grace's company for his last days.

'Have you had some success?' He picked up Grace's lead and continued the conversation. His father had been a stockman when Marcus had been young. He'd had to give that up when Marcus's mother had abandoned them but perhaps he remembered those days and, who knew, maybe he and his father would finally find some common ground with Grace's help.

Stranger things had happened. Grace had managed, in principle, to get support for the muster from the hospital and the transplant foundation but the local council was proving more difficult to persuade. 'Have you had the route approved yet?'

Grace shook her head. 'No. The council is being really stubborn. Even though we've offered to do the muster early on a Sunday they say they can't close the bridge to traffic. But they close the bridge for several hours for the New Year's Eve fireworks *and* for the running festival. They even had cows on it a few years ago for a fundraising breakfast but now they've decided it's too disruptive.'

'You've done your homework.'

'Of course I have.'

'Is it a financial issue? Road closures for major events are costly, and I imagine it's an even more expensive exercise to close the bridge.'

'You're not suggesting I bribe them?' She smiled and his mood lifted instantly.

'No, but you could offer to compensate them for their costs and time and effort. Call it a little sweetener.'

'But not a bribe?'

'No.'

She laughed. 'You probably have a good point but the muster is for a charity. I want to maximise the profits and it would annoy me to have to hand over good money after we'd worked so hard to raise it. Merridy has organised lots of sponsors, companies have been very generous, but I'm sure they would want their money going to the cause, not the council. They are the only sticking point.'

Marcus figured it was highly likely that the companies wouldn't care where their money went as long as they got some positive exposure and the tax benefits but that thought probably wasn't helpful at all. 'Have you considered alternative routes?'

Grace sighed. 'Merridy has her heart set on the bridge. It would bring massive publicity.'

'I don't disagree, but it might just not be possible.'

'Which stock route are you using?' Bill asked.

Grace and Marcus both looked at him in surprise. It was unusual for him to keep track of a conversation like this, particularly when it was occurring between two other people, but it seemed he had followed the topic after all.

'It's not technically a stock route,' Grace told him. 'We want to truck the cattle in to Sydney's north shore and walk them across the Harbour Bridge but the council is giving me grief. They say it can't be done.'

'Well, they're wrong.'

'What do you mean?'

'You're talking about the Sydney Harbour Bridge?'

'Yes.'

'It's a designated stock route,' Bill said.

'A what? How do you know that?'

'I am a drover. Stock routes are my bread and butter. Cattle need water, which means I need to know the stock routes and the watering holes. Not that I've ever needed to use the Harbour Bridge but I'm telling you, it's a stock route.'

Grace looked at Marcus. He shrugged. There was no way he'd take his father's word for it. But he could see Grace was getting excited.

'Are you saying I can request to walk the cattle over the bridge and the council will have to let me?' she asked Bill.

Bill frowned and shook his head and Marcus could feel Grace's disappointment. 'How many cattle are you talking about?'

Marcus wasn't sure if Bill was losing his train of thought but Grace went with him. 'I'm not sure. A few hundred hopefully. It depends on how many people want to be involved.'

'That might work. The stock route is not the whole bridge. It's only the pedestrian walkway so it will depend on the size of your herd.'

'That's better than nothing. In fact, that's the best news I've had all day. Thank you.' She stood up and gave Bill a big hug. He looked surprised but didn't resist. He was probably too taken aback to protest. Marcus couldn't remember ever hugging his father. Or his father ever hugging him. 'I'm going to go and do some digging right away,' Grace said.

Marcus followed her out of the room. She stopped outside the door and turned to him. Her face was alight, her amber eyes shining. 'Isn't that brilliant news?' she said. 'I just need to get that information confirmed and then the council will *have* to approve my request.'

'I don't want to rain on your parade, so to speak, and maybe it *was* a stock route once, but who knows if it still is?'

'Well, I intend to find out.'

'Don't you think that if what Bill is saying is true, the council would have told you?'

'They probably don't know. It must be years since anyone has tried to do what we're doing. I didn't mention stock routes.' She paused and gave him a considered look. 'You don't seem very enthusiastic.'

'I don't want you to get your hopes up. Do you think it's sensible to base your expectations on the ramblings of an alcoholic with dementia?'

'He seemed pretty certain.'

'You think he can remember a stock route from his droving days, which were thirty years ago, when he can't remember what he had for lunch?'

'You know that's how dementia works. Short-term memory is affected far more than long-term.'

'You think he can remember a stock route that he said he *never* used but he can't remember his own son? I was also there thirty years ago.'

Grace returned to her office. She had to investigate Bill's claim. She understood that Bill's unreliable memory was upsetting for Marcus. She knew how badly he wanted his father to remember him, to be able to give him the answers he was seeking, but she couldn't do anything about that. What she could do was follow Bill's lead.

She trawled the internet but her searches returned no results. She phoned the council but the person who it was recommended she speak to was away for the day. She left a message and decided she'd go back to see Bill at the first opportunity to see if he could tell her anything more. She didn't get a chance to get back to his room again that day and she was held up the following day too. It was after lunch before she got a moment to make the dash to his ward.

She almost collided with the empty meal trolley being wheeled along the corridor and she knew Bill's lunch would have already been delivered. She pushed open his door and was greeted by an empty room. Her heart plummeted. The bed had been stripped but there was no accompanying pile of clean linen indicating that someone was halfway through a task. Bill didn't have many personal effects dotted around the room but Grace had seen enough hospital rooms to know when someone was just out of bed or the room had been vacated. It could only mean one thing.

She backtracked to the nurses' station and glanced at the wall. The box next to room sixteen was empty. His name had been wiped from the board.

He was gone.

She was aware what that meant but she would check anyway. Maybe he had just been moved.

She was pleased to see that Tania was on duty. Grace wasn't Bill's family, she didn't need to be informed of what was going on, but, as a staff member, it was possible she'd be kept in the loop.

'Bill Washington?' She asked the question.

Tania shook her head. Nothing more needed to be said. He was gone.

'When?'

'About two o'clock this morning.'

'Was anyone with him?'

'Marcus was here.'

Marcus knew. And, once again, he hadn't said anything to her. What was the matter with him? Why did he insist on keeping everyone out? She had bared her soul to him, he knew everything about her, everything about her fears and her losses. Why couldn't he share anything with her?

She marched back to the renal ward and found him in his office, going through some papers. His door was open and she didn't bother knocking. If he thought she was just going to let this go he was very much mistaken. She closed the door behind her, making a poor attempt not to slam it. He looked up in surprise.

'Were you going to tell me?' She knew she should start with condolences but they were already way past that point.

'Tell you what?'

'About your father? Did you not think I'd

want to know?' She made sure to keep her tone neutral, even though she was furious with him and his refusal to share any personal thoughts or emotions with her.

'I knew you'd hear.'

'Well, maybe I wanted to hear about it from you.'

'Why?'

'Because he was your *father* and I thought you might be upset. I thought you might want some company. I would have come in to the hospital if you'd asked me to.' She tried to stay calm but her fiery temper was threatening to get the better of her.

'Grace, I'm fine. It's all okay.'

'How can you say that?'

'Bill hasn't been part of my life for a very long time and the man who was here wasn't even him.' He shrugged. 'Nothing has changed now he's gone.'

'But you wanted answers.'

'And I didn't get them and there's nothing I can do about that. So, can we move on?'

He returned his attention to the papers in front of him and it was obvious from his body language that he thought the discussion was over. Grace begged to differ.

His words had really hurt her. She knew this shouldn't be about her but how could he be so blasé? Was Bill's death really so insignificant to him? She worried that he was bottling things up and that frightened her. She had seen what happened when people buried their emotions and refused to acknowledge their issues—they became ticking time-bombs until one day they exploded.

Was he really so self-contained and self-sufficient?

She knew a little about his childhood and it really wasn't surprising he didn't confide in others or rely on their support but she wasn't just a colleague, neither was she just a friend. Surely she was more than that, wasn't she? Why wouldn't he talk to her? Did she mean nothing to him?

She needed to work out a way to make him talk to her. He had to be hurting and she wasn't going to ignore a friend in need. She'd made that mistake once before and she wouldn't do it again. She would make a dignified exit and deal with this later but as she walked towards the door Marcus's exasperated tone stopped her in her tracks.

'You're kidding me!'

Unsure if he was addressing her, she hesitated and turned back to him but he wasn't looking at her, he was still reading the papers.

'What is it?' The question was out of her mouth before she realised he probably wasn't about to share anything with her but to her amazement he looked up.

'The nursing home sent some of his papers over.' He held up the page he was reading. 'This is his funeral instructions. Apparently he wants to be cremated and have his ashes scattered on a plot of land he owns in Toowoomba.'

'Is that a problem?'

'I didn't know he had land there.'

Grace frowned. 'Does it make a difference?'

Marcus either chose to ignore her question or didn't know the answer. 'I guess I shouldn't be surprised. Even when he's dead, he's still keeping secrets.'

He might say that nothing had changed but Grace could see traces in him of the little boy he'd been, a boy looking for answers and look-ing for love. But she knew he'd never admit that.

She could love him if he'd let her.

'I'm sure you can arrange for someone else to do it for you if you prefer,' she said, her voice softening.

'His lawyer is also in Toowoomba. I'll have to have a meeting with him.'

Grace suspected that if Marcus really wanted to avoid Toowoomba he could arrange to meet the lawyer in Sydney if he offered to pay ex-penses. She didn't think money was an issue but she thought it would do him good to go back to Toowoomba. It might be a cleansing ex-perience, it might give him some closure. She suspected his memories of Toowoomba were far more onerous than the reality. Maybe he should face his demons. Maybe then he would finally get some perspective.

Memories could be powerful but experi-ence had taught her that at some point difficult memories needed to be confronted, otherwise they kept all the power, and she doubted that the memories of a twelve-year-old boy were terribly accurate. She didn't doubt they were powerful—they had shaped the last twenty years of his life, after all—but maybe it was time to take back control. He needed to address his issues rather than ignoring them, or they would only fester and grow.

Something had to be done to help him move on. He thought he was coping but Grace could see the weaknesses in his argument. If he was coping that well with everything that had happened in the past, then going back to Toowoomba wouldn't be the stumbling block it appeared to be.

She would help him.

'I'm going home to Toowoomba in a couple of weeks,' she told him. 'Why don't you come with me? We could do this together.' He looked at her and she knew he was going to make an excuse, to reject her suggestion, but she was certain it was a good one and she wasn't going to let him refuse to consider it. 'Think about it,' she added. 'You can let me know over the next day or so.'

CHAPTER EIGHT

SINCE BILL'S DEATH Marcus had thrown himself into work and retreated further into his shell. He couldn't admit that Bill's death had rattled him but it had spelt the end of his chances to get the answers he'd so desperately wanted. He'd avoided Grace, keeping their contact to a minimum, mainly so that he didn't have to talk about his feelings. She'd only be disappointed to find that they were of anger, frustration and disbelief rather than the more appropriate ones of sadness, loss and grief.

Grace had insisted on going to the funeral. He'd tried to talk her out of it—after all, she'd told him she hated funerals—but she hadn't been dissuaded. He'd settled on a private funeral that he'd let the war veterans' nursing home organise and in the end he gave in to Grace. Partly because her presence would distract from the fact that he couldn't be the grieving son everyone expected to see but mainly because, quite simply, he wanted her there.

The funeral had been bittersweet. Grace recounted stories Bill had told her from his droving days, painting a picture of a man Marcus had never known. Marcus himself had no stories to tell. No happy memories to share. He wondered if Grace had put on a brave face for him but he didn't reiterate that there was no need, he wasn't mourning, he'd lost his father a long time ago.

He didn't need his father and he didn't need Grace. He'd let her get much too close and it had been a mistake all along.

Though he didn't know how he was going to resolve the problem. He didn't know if he wanted to. And after two weeks of shutting her out, sitting next to her on the plane as they approached Toowoomba was doing his head in.

The irony of his situation wasn't lost on him. If he didn't need her, why had he accepted her suggestion that they fly back to Toowoomba together? He knew having her company would make it easier and she certainly was a distraction. He could smell her familiar floral shampoo and it made his head reel in longing. As she leant across him to pass her meal tray to the hostess her breast brushed against his arm and he just wanted to take her in his arms, hold her tight and forget about the rest of the world and his dysfunctional past.

The way she made him feel frightened him.

She made him feel as if he was worth something.

He had even found himself imagining having a future with her. Could he stay in Sydney? Could it work?

She made him believe he could be happy. That his past didn't matter. But he knew it did.

He wasn't good enough for her.

He should let her go before he disappointed her, he thought that was inevitable, but he couldn't let her go. Not yet. And so here he was, travelling to Toowoomba with Grace beside him.

Toowoomba. The last place on earth he ever thought he'd return to.

He grew increasingly nervous as they approached their destination. The funeral had been just one thing on the list of responsibilities. He had been going through the motions, ticking off the formalities and now, finally, he was able to embark on the final step of his duty. He jiggled his legs up and down and Grace reached across and held his hand. Her gesture was comforting but he was dismayed that he'd let her see his nervousness.

'It'll be okay,' she said. 'Are you sure you don't want some company at the lawyer's?'

'No. I don't want to think about it.' He had a meeting scheduled with Bill's lawyer to find out the details of the land Bill owned and to get other instructions. 'Tell me about your plans for the weekend.'

'It's my sister-in-law's birthday. That's why I'm coming home. There's a party at my brother's place tomorrow.'

'Is it a special birthday?'

'No. But this is Merridy, my sister-in-law who is organising the muster. After her transplant she said she's going to celebrate every birthday in style so I always make an effort to get back if I can. They run a feed lot so it's hard for them to get away. I always have to come to the party.

It's a good chance to catch up with everyone and I get to see my goddaughter as well.'

'You have a goddaughter?' Despite knowing that they'd spent far more time talking about her than him over the past few weeks, he still continued to discover new things about her. She was far more extroverted and social than he was and her family and friends were an important part of her life. He couldn't imagine anyone asking him to be a godparent for their child.

'Merridy's sister is my best friend from high school. Her daughter, Chloe, is my goddaughter.'

Her reply reminded him of one of the reasons he hated small towns and Toowoomba in particular. Everyone knew everyone and everything. There was no way people would have forgotten him. Grace hadn't. What the hell was he doing, going back?

The plane touched down and he stood and lifted the box containing Bill's ashes from the locker above his head. This was it. A weekend of memories and loneliness stretched before him.

Grace stood up. 'You're welcome to join us for

the party tomorrow,' she said, and for a moment the idea appealed as an alternative to a lonely, empty day before he registered that there would be way too many people from his past all together in one place. He was happy to see Grace but that happiness didn't extend to meeting her family again. He was already too involved. It was going to be difficult enough to walk away from Grace before he disappointed her without having to handle her family's criticism too.

He shook his head. 'Thank you, but I'm good.'

'You know I'm here for you if you need me.' Grace said as they prepared to part ways.

He could see her inherent traits of trust and honesty reflected in her amber eyes. Her world was black and white. So different from his. His was all shades of grey. The only bright light in his personal life was standing in front of him, offering to help.

He didn't deserve her. She was too good for him. 'I'll be fine.'

He'd let her brother Hamish collect her and he would pick up his hire car, see the lawyer and check into his hotel. He'd have dinner and read through some journal articles he hadn't had time to look at yet. He shook his head. His weekend was looking more depressing by the minute. He was tempted to change his mind. To race after Grace and ask her to go with him.

He could handle this, he told himself as he settled into the car. He plugged the lawyer's address into the navigation system and pulled into the light traffic as he tried to ignore the empty seat beside him.

Marcus had some time to kill before his appointment, so he switched off the navigation and drove through town, looking for the ghosts of his childhood. He drove past his old house but it had been demolished and a mansion had been built in its place. Most of the houses in the area had been renovated. There were lots of gracious Queenslanders, neat and well kept with their wraparound verandas and large blocks of land.

His old house was only a couple of streets from the primary school and close to the centre of town and, judging by the houses, he guessed the land values had gone up in the past twenty years. He turned the corner and drove past Grace's family home. He remembered it but hoped that no one would notice him drive by. He continued up the hill to Picnic Point. It was mid-morning on a Friday. There were a few mothers with young children in the park and a few older people who looked as though they'd just finished an exercise class, sitting having coffee.

He parked the car and walked to the lookout that took in the view over the ranges. Picnic Point was where teenagers came to hang out late on a Friday and Saturday night—it was a rite of passage once they got their driver's licences— but he had been long gone by then. Maybe he should have brought Grace with him. They could have parked the car and fooled around. It would certainly have kept his mind off the impending lawyer's appointment. He smiled, feeling a little bit brighter, and returned to the car.

He found a space in the main street right outside the lawyer's office. Some things may have changed, buildings had been demolished and new ones built in their place, but parking in a country town was still easy.

Marcus introduced himself to the receptionist, still in some measure of disbelief that he was actually back in Toowoomba.

He was ushered into the office. Charles Mc-Donald stood up behind his desk. He was in his late fifties, Marcus guessed, and extended his hand in greeting as he said, 'My condolences about Bill.'

Marcus assumed he knew about his estrangement from his father but the lawyer had the courtesy not to mention it and allowed Marcus to get down to business without engaging in small talk.

Marcus's first order of the meeting was to get the details regarding the block of land. He was anxious to scatter Bill's ashes. In his mind it would take him one step closer to the end and he was in a hurry to get there.

'It's a bit more than a block,' Charles informed him, 'and there's the will to be read. You are the sole beneficiary.'

'Of what?'

'Bill's estate.'

Marcus hadn't expected Bill to have anything to leave behind. He knew his father had had a pension and enough money to live on. He had topped up Bill's account via a monthly direct debit. It had been his way of assuaging guilt for not visiting him. Ever.

'It's not extensive, just the land and some money in the bank,' Charles said as he handed a piece of paper to Marcus. He looked at the figures in surprise. It was clear from the balance that Bill had never touched a cent of Marcus's money. All of his money would be coming back to him. With interest.

That made Marcus smile. Maybe he and his father had had something in common after all. Both could be stubborn bastards. So certain that they knew best.

'I don't want it,' he said. He wanted nothing from his father. Nothing except answers and it was too late for those.

'It's yours but what you choose to do with it is also up to you,' Charles explained. 'You can donate the money, set up a trust for future generations and sell the land. The neighbours might be willing to buy it. They made an offer once before but Bill wasn't able to give instructions so I had to turn it down. It was a fair offer. You could see if they are still interested.'

'Do you have their details?'

'I do. This is the address of your land and these are the neighbour's details.' He slid two more pieces of paper across the desk to Marcus. 'Lachlan and Merridy Gibson.'

Marcus tried to hide his surprise. Nothing about this whole process should surprise him any more but Bill just kept on delivering curve balls.

'There's also a file with some letters and personal effects that Bill left with me,' Charles said as he handed Marcus a slim box file. 'Have a look through it all and if you have any questions give me a call.'

Marcus took the file and pulled out the title of the land along with the map. With no other commitments for the day he decided he would drive out to see the block. It would give him time to think.

The wide tree-lined streets of town gave way to the familiar small hills and valleys filled with eucalypts and tea trees. He had his window down and the air temperature dropped as he drove north-west. He could smell rain and saw clouds gathering in the distance. The change looked far enough away and he hoped it would hold off until he'd seen the property. He drove past a wide dirt driveway bisected by a cattle grid and noticed a sign nailed to the wooden fence post—*'L&M Gibson'*. His neighbours. Grace's brother. He kept driving.

His driveway was another five kilometres along the road, the entry marked with a sign that simply listed the lot number. The fences appeared in reasonable condition and a metal gate restricted entry. He unlocked the chain around the gate with the key Charles had given him, pushed it open and drove onto the property. His property.

He drove around, following rutted tyre tracks, getting a feel for the land. From what he could see, it appeared he'd inherited several hectares of prime land. He shook his head. His father might not have known how to raise a son but he knew about cattle and what they needed to thrive. None of this made sense.

He completed a circuit of the property before he eventually parked beside a creek bed. Taking Bill's ashes, he scattered them under one of the willow trees, honouring him in death as he'd been asked to. The air was still and heavy as he let go of his final link to his family. It was a fitting end to his father's life, he felt. Bill had lived a solitary existence, so it seemed right that it should end this way. Just one person there to mark the occasion. As the last of the ashes drifted to the ground he wondered who would be at his own funeral one day. Who would he leave behind? Was he more like his father than he wanted to admit?

Marcus shook his head. There was no way of knowing what the future would bring.

He returned to the car and put the empty box in the boot beside the box of papers that Charles had given him. He took out the file and sat in the car, flicking through the documents and growing increasingly disturbed by the information before him.

When he finished he returned the papers to the file. He'd been given yet more questions and fewer answers but at least this time he had an idea of where to begin looking for them. He started the car and returned to town.

* * *

The rain had come and gone as he visited the local council offices and searched the internet. Finally, he had unearthed some answers to his questions and now he was more determined than ever to make sure he had no reason to return to Toowoomba. He was done with this town.

He would tidy up the loose ends and make sure he never had to set foot here again, he thought as he knocked on the door of Grace's brother's house.

The door opened and a streak of red fur dashed out through the gap and darted around Marcus's legs. Reg nudged his wet nose into Marcus's palm, seeking attention. Marcus recognised the cattle dog and patted him automatically as the door opened wider.

'Marcus! How did you know I was here?'

He looked up from the dog into Grace's amber eyes and his heart lifted immediately at the sight of her. She was a sight for sore eyes or, more aptly, for a sore heart and he longed to take her in his arms and let her distract him from his troubles, but she wasn't the person he'd expected to see. 'I didn't. I came to speak to your brother. Isn't this his house?'

Grace nodded. 'Yes, but I don't know where he is. What did you want to see him for?'

'The block of land my father owns shares a boundary with this property. The lawyer said that Lachlan and Merridy had made Bill an offer but he hadn't accepted it. I wanted to know if they were still interested.'

'The land is yours now? He left it to you?'

'Yes.'

'And you're going to sell it?' She frowned as she spoke.

'Of course. What else would I do with it? I don't need a block of land in Toowoomba.' Despite the fact that Toowoomba had changed, it still didn't hold happy memories for him. Despite what he'd discovered today, he still wanted nothing to do with his father or what he'd left for him. 'I never want to come back here again. I want nothing to do with the place.'

Grace stepped back and opened the door wider. 'You'd better come in. Lachlan's not here but I'll introduce you to Merridy.'

Merridy was in the large, farmhouse-style

kitchen, which had been extended to open out into a large living space that overlooked the paddocks.

'Merridy, this is Marcus Washington. He's a nephrologist doing a temporary stint at Kirribilli General but his dad was Bill Washington.'

Merridy had an apron tied around her waist and wiped her hands before shaking his. 'Was?'

'He died a couple of weeks ago,' Marcus told her.

'I'm sorry to hear that.'

'Marcus has inherited Bill's land.'

'The land next to us?' She directed her question at Marcus.

'Yes. Bill's lawyer told me you and Lachlan had made an offer to purchase it once before. I wondered if you were still interested.'

'You want to sell?'

'I do.'

'Lachlan will be back shortly, in time for dinner. You're welcome to stay and eat with us,' she said. 'We can discuss it then.'

'Thank you but no. Perhaps the two of you could talk it over and see if you're still interested. I'll leave you my number.'

'We're definitely interested. It's a great piece of land.'

Marcus pulled out a business card and wrote his mobile number on it before handing it to Merridy.

'Are you okay?' Grace asked as she walked with him back to his car, Reg at their heels. 'What else happened at the lawyer's? What else did he tell you?'

'What makes you think he told me anything else?'

'You're edgy. Unsettled. Something has upset you.'

He was all of those things. Usually that would make him retreat until he had sorted through his problems. On his own. He would have gone for a surf or ridden his horse until his mind cleared but he had neither of those options here. All he had was Grace. But she was enough. She listened well and without judgement. She had proven herself to be a good, impartial listener and he really didn't fancy more of his own company.

'Do you want to go for a drive with me?' he asked.

'Sure.' She didn't hesitate. Unlike him, she never seemed to overanalyse things. She took things at face value. Trusting. Easy. 'Just let me put Reg inside and tell Merridy so she doesn't think you've abducted me.'

She was gone only a few minutes but returned with a picnic basket and a blanket.

'What's that for?' he asked as he reached out and took the basket from her.

'Merridy said you looked like you needed to eat. It's a beautiful evening, it seems a shame to waste it. Do you feel like a picnic?'

'Why not?' he replied, realising he'd go just about anywhere with her. His spirits had lifted in the last ten minutes alone.

'Where do you want to go?'

'I have no idea.'

'Would you take me to see your land? There has to be a spot for a picnic there.'

For a lack of any better ideas he took her suggestion. For the second time today he parked beside the creek, near the willows. The sun was dipping below the hills and the sky, clear now after the rain, was turning pink but the air was still warm.

'This is beautiful,' Grace said as she spread the picnic blanket under a willow. She looked around and took in the scenery. She breathed in deeply and sank down onto the rug. 'Did you scatter Bill's ashes?'

'Yes. Why do you ask?'

'I thought this looked like a good place if you hadn't done it already.'

He smiled, wondering why it was he only seemed to smile when Grace was around. He hadn't thought he would smile at all today but, once again, she was making everything better. 'This is the spot I chose,' he told her. 'I scattered them under that willow just over there.'

'It's perfect.' She reached out a hand and pulled him down beside her on the blanket. He set the picnic basket down and Grace opened it and assembled a platter of cheese, pâté, bread and cold meats.

He opened a bottle of wine and poured Grace a glass when she nodded in response to his gesture. He took a bottle of water for himself and said, 'Merridy got all this organised in the few minutes that you were inside?'

Grace smiled. 'It's the country way. She always seems to have food ready to go. She's a good organiser. The muster is in excellent hands.'

'How are things going with that?' he asked, but Grace shook her head as she cut a piece of cheese.

'We're not going to talk about that today. It can wait. Have something to eat and tell me what the lawyer said that's bothering you.'

'He didn't say anything. But he had a box of papers that Bill had left with him for safekeeping. To be passed onto me.'

'What was in there?'

'It was partly what *wasn't* in there. All the things you would expect were there—Bill's legal documents, his birth certificate, his passport, property titles, his will, but there was no marriage certificate.' Marcus felt like he was never going to get to the end of his search for answers. Every time he discovered one thing it led to two more questions, meaning he still had more questions than answers. 'Apparently, they were never married.'

'Does it matter?' She had a puzzled expression in her amber eyes but he could see the exact moment when one thought led to another. She was easy to read, her expressions open and honest, just like she was. There was nothing guarded about her, so totally different from him. 'You said you looked for her. Do you think that's why you never found her? Were you looking for her as a Washington?'

He nodded. 'It would have been helpful to have had this information years ago. I never knew her maiden name either. I don't know why Bill never gave these papers to me before. I don't know why he kept the information from me and now I'll never know.'

'Are you going to look for her again?'

'I have,' he admitted. 'And I've found her.'

'Already!' Grace's amber eyes glowed in the soft light of the evening and her fiery red hair shone, reflecting the rays of the setting sun. She looked beautiful and her expression was full of expectation. Marcus knew she was thinking he had good news to share but it was far from that.

'I could have found her a lot sooner if I'd been given these pieces of the puzzle before today.'

'Where is she? What are you going to do?'

'Nothing.'

'What do you mean, "nothing"?'

'She's dead.'

'What? No! What happened?'

'There was also a letter in with Bill's things.'

'I'm not following you. What letter? A letter to you?'

'No. A letter from my mother to Bill. A letter she wrote to him after she left.'

'What did it say?'

'She'd had an affair. She told Bill she had fallen in love with someone else and she was leaving to be with him. Knowing they were never legally married meant she could just walk out. But she didn't take me with her.'

'Did she say why?'

'She said her boyfriend didn't want to take on another man's child. She said she would work something out and come back for me. But she never did.'

'Maybe she died before she could come back.'

'No. That wasn't it. She married that man and changed her name. In the letter she gave her new name and address. My father never shared that information with me. For years I'd been looking for a person who didn't actually exist. But today I did a search for her online. She died when I was eleven. Five years after she left me. Five years after she said she'd come back for me. She had time to do it if she'd really wanted me.'

The details in the letter confirmed that his mother had abandoned him, rejected him. She'd never come for him even though she'd had the opportunity to do so. The contents of the letter had shocked and upset him. He hadn't thought anyone could upset him more than his father had but today he'd discovered that his mother had been the cause of all his angst. He'd blamed his father all this time, assumed Bill must have done something that had pushed his mother away. He hadn't been able to forgive his father when he'd been alive and had blamed him for his awful childhood, but now he'd found out Bill hadn't been the only one to blame.

'I don't know whether Bill loved her or loathed her. Was that why he drank? We never spoke about her. Was I a reminder of her? Did he send me away because he couldn't stand the sight of me?'

Grace put her wine glass down and knelt between his legs. She took his hands in hers and held onto them. He let her hold him. It comforted him. 'Maybe he couldn't cope on his own but whatever their reasons your parents made their own choices. Whatever they did was their decision. Their responsibility. You are not responsible for their actions. You were a child. You are the victim in this.'

Maybe she was right. It was his history but maybe it wasn't his fault. And as his history maybe it was time he put it behind him. He kept trying to tell himself he wasn't that boy any more. That boy who had grown up unloved and unwanted. Maybe it really was time to let him go.

He sighed. 'They're both dead. This is it. The end of the line. Both of them are gone now. I know as much as I'll ever know.'

'Is it enough?'

It wasn't nearly enough but it was all he would have. 'It will have to be. So now I have to put it all behind me.' Like he'd done before. He knew he would mentally box the information up and quite possibly refuse to think about it any further. 'What's done is done.'

'Is there anything I can do?' she asked.

She was curled between his legs. Her shirt was untucked and he could see a sliver of bare skin beneath the hem. He slid his fingers under her shirt and rested his hand on the warm skin of her stomach.

Dusk was settling over the land, a warm breeze stirred the branches of their willow tree and frogs called out to each other, their sound replacing the chatter of birds. He felt as though they were miles from civilisation. His fingers slid higher on Grace's belly until he reached the swell of her breast. He slipped his hand inside the cup of her bra and felt her nipple peak as he ran his finger across it.

Grace sighed and shifted between his thighs. Her eyes closed and her lips parted and he decided he'd spent enough time for one day sifting through the past and trying to find answers that were probably not there. Here, under the willows, on the banks of the creek they were a million miles away from other people and that was just how he liked it. He could forget about everything that had happened today and focus on Grace. She made him feel calm and content.

She made him feel happy. He knew it wouldn't last, nothing good ever lasted in his personal life, but he decided he'd enjoy it while he could.

He bent his head and kissed her. He would lose himself in her and everything would seem better. At least, for a while.

CHAPTER NINE

'MERRIDY SAID TO tell you that things are just about ready inside.' Grace spoke to her brother as she stepped outside to the barbeque.

'No worries,' Lachlan said as he turned the chicken skewers. 'Can I ask you something? Do you think Marcus is really serious about selling his land to us?'

She and Lachlan had discussed Marcus's offer over coffee the night before. Merridy and their parents had been there for the conversation too and Grace had filled them in on some of the details of Marcus's past twenty years but had kept the details about her personal involvement with him negligible. She figured all her family needed to know was that they worked together. She'd seen her mother and Merridy exchanging glances and wondered if they could see something in her face or hear it in her voice but if they suspected she was editing the story they didn't press her for further information.

'He's serious,' she replied. Lachlan should be having this conversation with Marcus, not her. It wasn't her business and she really didn't know much. But while she'd invited Marcus to the party a second time he'd, unsurprisingly, not accepted. She knew he wasn't overly comfortable in social situations and she knew he was even more unsettled by being back in Toowoomba. He had a lot of stuff to sort through, and she understood that, but that didn't stop her wishing he'd accepted her invitation. It might have done him good to be surrounded by a bit of normality or, at least, what passed as normality in the Gibson family.

'He doesn't want anything to do with Toowoomba,' she added, 'and considering he lives in Perth, what would he do with the land?'

If she had, even briefly, entertained the notion that things could become serious between them she knew the way Marcus felt about Toowoomba would be problematic. While she didn't plan on living here, she did visit regularly. She was inextricably tied to the town.

Her family was here. In a way it was still home for her but Marcus felt very differently about it and she didn't think he was likely to change his mind. He'd gone just about as far away from here as was possible without leaving the country. He'd said he was finished with Toowoomba and she believed him.

Time hadn't healed his wounds as it had done for her. Maybe now that he had closure over his mother's disappearance he would find peace, if not forgiveness. She hoped so.

'We made an offer to Bill a few years ago,' Lachlan said, 'but his lawyer turned it down. I don't want to start the process again if it's just a hypothetical.'

Grace might wish she could help Marcus but she knew he needed to release his emotions, willingly, before he'd be able to move on. In the meantime, perhaps she could help by assisting him to divest himself of his land. It seemed to be what he wanted. 'Marcus told me that the sale didn't go ahead because Bill wasn't in a sound frame of mind and his will stipulated that Marcus would inherit the land so the lawyer had to reject your offer. The lawyer had power of attorney. If Marcus had had it, he would have sold it to you then. But he's meeting a property valuer there today. He means business.'

Knowing Marcus was literally next door made her wish even more that he'd accepted her invitation. But she hadn't wanted to push it. She hadn't wanted to pressure him into doing something he might not enjoy.

'Good to know. Can you let Merridy and Mum know I'll be done in ten minutes?' Lachlan asked as he put the steaks on the grill.

Lillian was in the kitchen when Grace went back inside.

'Lachlan will be done in ten,' Grace told her mother. 'Where's Merridy?'

'Gone to get some paracetamol, she said she had a bit of a headache.' Lillian glanced at the microwave clock. 'She's been gone a while—do you want to check on her? I'd hate for her to miss her own party.'

Merridy and Lachlan's bedroom door was ajar. Grace knocked and pushed it open. Her sister-in-law was lying on the bed.

'Are you okay?' Grace asked.

Merridy opened her eyes. 'I think I might be coming down with something. I've had a bit of a headache all day,' she said as she sat up. 'Oh.' She put a hand to her temple.

'What is it?'

'My headache's worse.'

'Do you want me to get you something stronger than a paracetamol?'

'No. I can't take anything stronger.' Merridy looked at Grace. 'We were going to tell everyone at lunch but I'll tell you now. I'm pregnant.'

'That is so exciting! Congratulations.' Grace hugged her gently, taking care not to jostle her too much. She knew that Lachlan and Merridy had been hoping for this and that they'd had to put their baby plans on hold while Merridy recovered from her kidney transplant. 'Do you think this is morning sickness?'

'No. I'm twelve weeks, it's almost passed. This feels like a virus.'

'Have you got a temperature?' She put her hand on Merridy's forehead but that felt normal. 'Do you want to see a doctor?'

'No. I'm sure it'll pass. Just give me ten more minutes to see if the painkillers work.'

'I think it would be a good idea to get someone else's opinion. Why don't I get Dad or Hamish?' Grace's gut was telling her there was more going on here than just a virus. Merridy's colour wasn't quite right and she seemed a little vague. Her father was a doctor, and Hamish was a paramedic. Merridy's transplant meant she was prone to infections and now that she was pregnant Grace was uncomfortable ignoring her symptoms. A second opinion couldn't hurt.

She ducked out of the room to look for the others. She found Hamish first.

'Hame, can you find Dad, and ask him if he's got his medical bag in the car? I want him to check Merridy's BP.' Grace knew that, being a country GP, her father rarely went anywhere without his bag, which contained all the essentials for home visits and emergencies. He'd have his sphygmomanometer in there.

Grace went back to Merridy. She was lying down again and Grace made her stay supine until Hamish and her father appeared. Grace quickly recounted Merridy's symptoms and the fact she was expecting, but there wasn't time to celebrate the news before she sent Hamish off again to fetch Lachlan while George wrapped the cuff around Merridy's arm and listened for her heartbeat.

'One fifty-five over one hundred and four. You need to go to hospital,' George announced as Grace's brothers entered the room.

'Do you want me to call a crew?' Hamish asked.

'We can drive her,' George replied. 'We'll be just as fast as the ambulance if we go now.'

Lachlan's face was drained of colour and Grace knew he was desperately worried. Merridy was almost oblivious to what was going on around her now. Happy just to let other, more qualified people make the decisions for her. 'We've got this,' Grace told Lachlan. 'You've got a doctor, a nurse and a paramedic here and I'll call Marcus too. She'll be okay.'

Grace sent Lachlan with Hamish, their father and Merridy. The rest of the family followed and Grace called Marcus as the convoy departed.

'Marcus. I need a favour,' she said when he answered. 'It's Merridy, my sister-in-law, the one who had the kidney transplant. She's not well. Her BP is dangerously high—one fifty-five over one hundred and four—and we've just found out she's twelve weeks pregnant. We're taking her to the hospital. Can you meet us there?'

Marcus made good time and pulled into the hospital car park, where he found Grace waiting for him by the emergency entrance.

'They've just taken Merridy inside,' she said as she greeted him with a hug.

Marcus was surprised by her greeting. They hadn't been publicly affectionate, and he never was, but he could see by Grace's expression that she was upset and realised the hug was for her own sake. He hugged her back, hoping that in some small way he could make her feel better.

'Thank you for coming,' she said as she released him, 'I know Dad will make sure she gets the proper attention but it can't hurt to have your opinion too. You're the expert.'

'Who is her nephrologist?' he asked, switching quickly into his professional persona. He was far more comfortable in that role.

'Elliot.'

Good. Knowing Merridy's specialist personally would make things easier, he thought as fell into step beside Grace. He would assess Merridy and then place a call to Elliot if necessary.

Grace stopped next to the triage desk and introduced him to her father. 'Dad, this is Marcus. Marcus, my dad, George.'

'We've got you on Merridy's paperwork as the consulting specialist,' George said as he shook Marcus's hand. There was no time and no need for Marcus to be nervous, they were just two doctors with Merridy as their focus. 'And I've sorted your visitation rights.'

Marcus nodded but didn't bother asking if everyone was happy to have him treat Merridy. Grace was right. He was the expert when it came to nephrology. This episode of hypertension might be completely unrelated to Merridy's transplant but his opinion was still worthwhile. Her transplant could not be ignored and treatment needed to be administered accordingly but also needed to take into account the fact that she was in the early stages of a pregnancy. 'Where is Merridy?'

'They've just taken her into a bay.'

Marcus cleared the cubicle of people, with the exception of Lachlan and the nurse who was hooking Merridy up to the monitors. He got Merridy's medical history from Lachlan as he waited for the monitors to start giving him the information he needed. No temperature, oxygen sats normal but BP dangerously high. According to Lachlan, when they'd seen Merridy's obstetrician a week ago her BP had been fine.

He ordered blood tests, looking in particular for infection of the kidneys or urinary tract, started medication for hypertension and got the nurse to hook up a saline drip. He put a call in to Elliot and also to Merridy's obstetrician, who confirmed Lachlan's recall, before going out to speak to Merridy's family. Lachlan didn't look as though he was capable of remembering the information so it was easier for Marcus to inform the family himself.

The waiting room was bursting at the seams and he was surprised and a little overwhelmed to find that most of the people there were Merridy and Lachlan's family. The entire party seemed to have relocated to the hospital.

'Other than high blood pressure, everything else looks normal so far,' he said reassuringly. 'She doesn't have a temperature, which is a good sign, but I'm running some tests for infection and started her on methyldopa to bring her BP down. You may remember, high blood pressure is a common side-effect of anti-rejection medication so this isn't unusual to see, but her pregnancy is a complicating factor.'

Merridy would need careful monitoring even once her BP normalised as women who developed hypertension in their first trimester were twice as likely to develop pre-eclampsia than other women, but Marcus would let Merridy's obstetrician deal with that. His job was just to get things under control for now. 'The medication may take a few days to work so I'll get her admitted overnight. The hospital staff have my number and will let me know when the test results come back. Her GP should be able to manage things from here on but I will check on her in the morning before we go back to Sydney.'

Grace was shaking her head. 'I'm going to change my flight,' she said. 'I'll take a couple of days' leave and stay here. I can't go back now.'

He waited while everyone thanked him for his help, even though he was anxious to escape.

He headed for the car park but, aware he was being followed, he stopped walking and turned around. Grace's mother was behind him. She hadn't called to him, hadn't said anything, but he knew she wanted to speak to him. Why else would she be there?

She was an older version of Grace. The same petite build, her hair a slightly faded shade of red, the same amber eyes and with a few more lines. He experienced a flash of familiarity. Did he remember her or was he just seeing what Grace would look like in another thirty years?

'Thanks for your help,' she said as he stopped walking. 'I know my family would have managed but it's hard when the patient is a relative. We appreciate your expertise.'

'Don't mention it.' Marcus felt uncomfortable. Out of the confines of the hospital he was awkward and uneasy. He was eager to get away but it was obvious she had more to say.

'I also wanted to pass on our condolences about your father.' She hesitated and then continued, 'It seems wrong just to let it go unsaid, despite the circumstances.'

Marcus nodded. 'Thank you. It may have been a blessing in disguise, I'm not sure how much living he was doing.'

'Grace said his dementia was very bad. We hadn't seen him for several years. I didn't know he had deteriorated that badly.'

'You knew Bill?' Marcus couldn't reconcile the man he knew having had much to do with anyone in Toowoomba.

Lillian nodded. 'He was a patient of George's and I was the practice nurse. We knew your father.'

'And me?'

'Of course. But it's been a long time. I feel responsible for that.'

Marcus frowned. 'For what?'

'For sending you to Perth.'

'What are you talking about?'

'I was the one who rang your aunt. I was the reason she took you to Perth.'

'You?' It took Marcus a moment to process what he was hearing. What exactly was Grace's mother saying? 'I don't understand.'

'I phoned your aunt. Your father's...health was deteriorating rapidly.' Marcus could hear Lillian choosing her words carefully. 'The school had notified authorities and there were concerns for your welfare. We did what we could, bringing meals over and doing washing, but your father was...difficult. I was worried that you would be put into foster care and I didn't think that was a good solution, not even in a small town, and I knew you had other family. Your aunt was listed as your father's next of kin and so I called her. But I never imagined that my actions would mean it would be twenty years before you would see your father again.'

Marcus had wanted answers but this revelation was completely unexpected.

He needed to think.

'Thank you for telling me.' Lillian's admission reminded him that everyone in town knew everyone else's business. Reminded him of why he wanted to stay as far away from Toowoomba as possible. Although things had changed in twenty years, they hadn't changed enough for him. 'If you'll excuse me, I need to go.'

Lillian wasn't responsible for the fact that he hadn't seen his father for twenty years, he alone had made that choice. But it had always been based on the idea that his father had sent him away and apparently that hadn't been the case. Although there could be no denying that his father hadn't taken care of him while he had still been living with him. His father had chosen alcohol over his son and Marcus couldn't blame Lillian for trying to help him. She might have instigated getting him out of Toowoomba but this hadn't been the place for him anyway. It hadn't been at twelve and it wasn't now.

He didn't belong here. Not in Toowoomba and not with Grace's extended family. All these people were here for Merridy and the same people would be here for Grace if she needed them. But he had no one. He needed to leave. He didn't fit in with her world. And he would never belong.

* * *

'Grace, you need to come back to Sydney. Marcus is leaving.'

Grace had mentally replayed the conversation she'd had with Lola for the entire flight home from Toowoomba. Marcus had given notice and was leaving a few weeks before his time was up. If Grace didn't get home on the next available flight, she risked missing him altogether.

She couldn't understand what was going on. She'd called and left messages. He'd texted back but his messages had been impersonal—'Pleased to hear Merridy's doing better', 'Connie says hello'—and there was no sign of the intimacy she'd thought they'd so recently shared. No exchanges of confidences and never a hint that he was planning on leaving early. Part of her hoped Lola was wrong. Perhaps the hospital grapevine had made a mistake, but the chances were good that Lola knew something so Grace was returning to Sydney as quickly as she could.

Lola collected her from the airport and dropped her at Marcus's apartment block. She managed to get into the building as someone else left and she caught the lift to his floor. As she pressed the doorbell for his apartment she shifted her weight nervously from foot to foot. What if she'd missed him?

She couldn't believe he hadn't told her or that he'd been going to leave without saying goodbye. She had been so confident that they were building something worthwhile, had felt as if she was slowly peeling back his layers, that he was starting to share some of his feelings and emotions with her. Grace knew about the issues he'd had with his father and that he felt abandoned by his mother. She wasn't sure if she'd ever get him to reveal his whole self, she knew he had a lot to deal with and was still hurting, but she'd thought she was helping. She'd thought he trusted her.

Grace blamed herself. Her family. Her mother had told her of the conversation she'd had with Marcus. Was that why he was leaving Sydney early? Was it narcissistic to think it was all because of her?

He answered the door and Grace's heart gave a little flip. She hadn't thought it would be possible but in the week since she'd seen him she'd forgotten just how handsome he was and he almost took her breath away. He was clean-shaven and dressed in light cotton pants and a red T-shirt. He looked gorgeous.

'Grace. I wasn't expecting you.' His tone was flat and her heart plummeted. This hadn't been the greeting she'd been hoping for.

'Can I come in?' He hesitated and she was tempted to put her foot in the door in case he tried to close it. She wasn't going to let him leave without some sort of explanation. 'Lola told me you're going back to Perth early.'

He didn't deny that her information was correct. He stepped back and made room for her to pass.

'Is it because of me?' she asked bluntly. She didn't want to make it all about her but what other reason could there be for his abrupt departure? Honesty was important to him. Was that what this was about? Did he think she'd lied to him? Kept secrets from him that she should have shared?

'I had no idea my mother had had any role to play in removing you from your father. You can't think I wouldn't have told you that if I knew,' she said. 'My mother feels terrible. She feels responsible for you not going back to see your father.'

'It's not because of you. One of the nephrologists at the Queen Victoria Hospital in Perth has been diagnosed with pancreatic cancer. He's resigned from his position to spend time with his family. I'm going back to Perth to take over his caseload.'

'This has nothing to do with what happened last week, then? With my mother?'

He shook his head. 'This has nothing to do with what happened last week or twenty years ago and even that wasn't your mother's fault. I've spoken to my aunt. I would have been removed from Bill's care with or without your mother's involvement.

'According to my aunt, I never asked why I was in Perth. I just assumed Bill sent me away and I barely spoke about him after that. I never asked to see him and my aunt never made me visit. I doubt our relationship would have been any better if I'd stayed in Toowoomba. Losing his son wasn't enough to get Bill to sort out his life and that has nothing to do with your mother. There's no denying my life would have been different if I'd stayed in Toowoomba but your mother's actions meant I went to family and got opportunities I would never have got otherwise. I have a lot to be grateful for. This isn't her fault.'

Grace wanted to believe him but she sensed there was more to this than he was telling her. She wanted to know what that was but as she was trying to work out if she dared press him for more information she saw a suitcase in his bedroom, a laptop bag leaning against it. He was halfway out the door.

'You're leaving today?'

He nodded.

'That's it?' she said. 'You're not coming back?'

'No.'

He didn't apologise. He didn't say he'd miss her or invite her to go with him. He'd said his reason for going wasn't anything to do with her but she wondered if there was something more she could do, some way of making him stay. She almost asked him to take her too.

She realised that for their relationship to work he needed to be shown commitment, trust, love and respect but he had to offer those things in return. She wanted him to consider her. To want her. To need her.

But perhaps he didn't share the same feelings for her that she did for him.

Who was she kidding? It was perfectly apparent that he didn't.

She should tell him how she felt but she couldn't bring herself to. She couldn't bring herself to give him all of her as it was quite likely she would get nothing in return.

She had to set him free. Set them both free. If he didn't realise on his own that they were meant to be together, she couldn't force it on him. She'd tried to give him happiness but it seemed it was out of her control. He had to find it on his own.

She was prepared to stick with him through thick and thin but he had to be prepared to do the same. He deserved to be loved and she could do that. She loved him with all her heart but she needed his love in return.

And that was the crux of the problem. She'd done the one thing she hadn't planned on doing. The one thing she'd known would end in heartbreak. She'd fallen in love with him. And he was walking away from her without even a backward glance.

She swallowed her pride, her tears and her heartache. She hugged him and wished him happiness in the future, and then she left. She couldn't let him see her tears. This time they were all for herself.

Marcus sat on the front veranda of his house near Margaret River. It was one of the few shacks that was still in almost original condition but its lack of modern amenities was superbly compensated for by its position. He could see the ocean from where he sat and could check out the surf conditions from his front door. He'd gone for a surf at first light and had not long returned.

This was usually his favourite time of the day, it was calm and peaceful, but today he felt lonely. He had never felt lonely until he'd met Grace. Until he'd started *missing* Grace. And he'd never felt lonely here before. Margaret River and this house was his sanctuary. Three hours south of the city, it was his escape and he loved it here. He had never shared this space with a woman but today he wished that Grace was here with him. Today he was missing her more than ever.

Leaving her was the hardest thing he'd ever done but at the time he'd thought it had been the right thing to do. He'd told her his reasons for leaving had had nothing to do with her family and he'd meant it, up to a point. It had had nothing to do with the past but everything to do with the future. Her family was at the centre of her world and he didn't belong there with them. He didn't know how to be a part of that life.

He would not be the kind of man her parents wanted for their only daughter. He wasn't enough for her. He couldn't be what she needed and he knew he would only disappoint her. She was better off without him. He wanted to be the person for Grace just as he knew she was the person for him, but he was terrified of letting her down. What did he know about love and commitment?

Marcus stared out at the ocean. The sea had always calmed him, given him a chance to think clearly and get perspective on his life, but he didn't like where his thoughts were heading today. Since leaving Sydney, he was being forced to face some harsh realities about himself. He'd always thought he had strength of character but now he was having doubts. Perseverance and persistence he had in spades when it came to his career, but he couldn't say the same about his relationships. He'd never had a serious relationship but whether that was due to a lack of desire for one or a lack of example to follow he didn't know. He'd certainly never wanted to try. Was that because he had an overwhelming fear of failure?

He didn't like to think like that of himself but he was worried it might be true. He'd told Grace he'd wanted answers from Bill and yet he'd been relieved to an extent when Bill's illness had made it impossible to have the difficult discussion. Had he deliberately left his visit too late? Knowing he would be able to blame a lack of communication for being unable to repair their relationship rather than blame himself?

He didn't want to leave things too late with Grace. He'd been getting too close to her and, afraid of failure, had left at the first opportunity. He had been afraid she wouldn't choose him.

This had nothing and everything to do with Grace.

She didn't need him, no one ever had, but he realised now that he desperately needed her. He'd been happy with her. And he hadn't been happy in a very long time. Maybe ever. In surgery he was content, satisfied with knowing he was good at his job. On his horse or his surfboard he was relaxed but neither of those pastimes could compare to how he felt when he was with Grace.

She'd told him to follow his heart. To be happy.

But he wasn't happy. He was lonely. And miserable.

Maybe he deserved it. Maybe it was genetic. His father had loved and lost. His father had been damaged and lonely. But he didn't want to end up like that.

Sitting on his veranda, contemplating his solitary existence, he knew he'd made a mistake. The reason to return to Perth had come at the perfect time, it had given him an opportunity to leave and he'd taken it, thinking it was the right thing to do, but then hindsight could be a terrible thing.

He'd definitely made a mistake. A huge one. It was his problem to deal with and he needed to fix it.

He missed her. He needed her. He wanted her. He loved her.

CHAPTER TEN

THE SKY WAS beginning to lighten in the east, a soft pale blue tinging the horizon, and Grace knew it wouldn't be long before the harbour would be bathed in the golden glow of a new dawn. It was going to be a beautiful crisp, clear, winter's day, perfect for the 'Herd across the Harbour' muster.

The crowds were already gathering and she could hear the soft snuffling of the cattle that Lachlan and his stockmen had corralled in the park. She loved the sound of the cattle. They were surprisingly quiet considering their size and they seemed calm and relaxed. She knew Lachlan had chosen beasts that were used to being around people and horses, had specifically selected them for their temperament, and they were all used to being haltered. They couldn't afford to have any animals go rogue on them.

She smiled. She almost still couldn't believe that she'd been able to pull this off and that Bill Washington had been right. The Sydney Harbour Bridge remained a dedicated stock route. After Bill had dropped his bombshell she'd discovered that, provided you paid a toll, stock could be taken across the bridge between midnight and six in the morning. She had wangled permission to start the muster at six on a Sunday but, given that it was expected to take about two hours to get all the animals and the people to the south side, the walkway would be cleared and open for regular foot traffic before nine. The official stock route was the eastern pedestrian walkway so, in theory, the bridge was open to traffic but the council had agreed to reduce the speed limit and close some lanes to separate the traffic from the muster and avoid spooking the animals. And now they were almost ready to start.

The muster had been a lifesaver for Grace over the past four weeks. The project had kept her busy outside work. Too busy to think about Marcus.

Almost too busy.

She and Lola had spent hours talking about Marcus—she was kidding herself if she thought he was going to be easy to forget.

She loved him. But obviously that wasn't enough.

She missed him and she hoped he was okay but he had made his decision and she had to get on with her life now.

She checked the time. Five thirty a.m.

News helicopters buzzed overhead and there were several news vans parked on the side of the road. One of the national morning television shows was doing their weather broadcast from the bridge and several reporters had signed on for the walk. The crowd of people numbered in the hundreds now and all participants should have checked in for registration. Some were walking and some had paid extra to ride. So far they had raised close to two hundred thousand dollars and the television morning show hosts would advertise the 'Herd across the Harbour' website so that viewers could also donate to the cause if they wished. Grace was committed to a short interview on camera prior to the start but she had time to do one more thing.

Each participant was able to write an individual message on a 'Herd across the Harbour' ribbon that would hang around their animal's neck, either their cow or their horse, and they could take that home with them, along with their commemorative T-shirt, at the conclusion of the event. Prior to the walk they were able to have their photographs taken with their beasts before professional stockmen led the animals across the bridge.

Grace knew that Marcus had sponsored an animal, donating a huge sum of money to the cause in Bill's name and almost doubling their previous fundraising efforts with his gift, and she wondered if he had sent instructions for a message to be written. She went in search of Lola, who was in charge of handing out the ribbons. If Marcus hadn't left instructions, maybe she would write a message in memory of Bill. After all, this event wouldn't have been possible, not in the way she and Merridy had imagined, without him.

She bumped into Connie and her parents and sister on her way to the official registration area. Connie was recovering well post-transplant and she was thrilled to be taking part in the muster. Grace hugged her and wished her well before continuing on to the registration desks. Merridy, whose blood pressure was once more back under control, was seated at one of the desks alongside Grace's mum. Her father and Hamish were also at the event, co-ordinating the first-aid volunteers. It was a real Gibson family affair but Grace wouldn't have it any other way.

She found Lola standing nearby, chatting to Hamish, with the remaining few ribbons draped over her arm. Considering it was five thirty in the morning, Lola looked amazing. Her skin glowed, she had curves in all the right places and her golden curls had that just-got-out-of-bed look that most men, as far as Grace could tell, couldn't resist, and that seemed to include her brother. Lola was touching Hamish's arm and he was hanging on her every word. He hadn't even noticed Grace's arrival.

Hamish's chiselled good looks would appeal to Lola too. Any good-looking man was on her radar and even though he was her brother Grace knew women found Hamish attractive.

She wondered who had introduced them or had Lola recognised him from all the family photos Grace had displayed in their flat?

She wanted to warn Hamish that Lola was a serial flirt but she knew they would both laugh at her, and although Lola had had more lovers than Grace could count, she thought there was no way Lola would actually sleep with Hamish. Sleeping with your best friend's brother would be weird. So what harm could come of a little casual flirting?

She cleared her throat as she casually stepped between them. She didn't want to lecture them but that didn't mean she had to encourage them. 'Haven't you got something better to do than flirt with my best friend?' Grace teased her brother.

'Dad has everything under control,' was his response, although Grace noticed he barely took his eyes off Lola as he replied.

Grace didn't doubt that their father would be running a tight ship and it seemed Hamish had no intention of budging. She rolled her eyes and turned to Lola instead.

'I'm just wondering if Marcus sent any instructions for the wording on his ribbon?' she asked her.

'No. Would you like to write something?'

Grace hesitated. She knew what she wanted to write but would Marcus think it was appropriate?

'I don't think he'd mind,' Lola said with a smile as she handed Grace a ribbon and a marking pen.

Grace leant on the table and printed on the ribbon.

In memory of Bill Washington
1951-2018

Then, with a quick backward glance to find that Hamish and Lola were still chatting animatedly, she went to find a spare cow to claim for Marcus. She had too many things to do this morning to worry about Hamish and Lola. Besides, Hamish was only here overnight and Lola was working later. How much trouble could they get into in the next few hours?

She paused for a moment, thinking of both Bill and Marcus as she hung the ribbon around the cow's neck. She had a sense of being watched but as she looked around the crowd she realised everyone was too busy with their own experience to be interested in her. She gave one last thought to Marcus. It was three in the morning in Perth so he would be in his bed, not thinking about her, but her jealous streak hoped that he would at least be alone.

She spoke to the stockman who was responsible for a handful of cows, including this one, and asked him to meet her at the front of the herd before she went to check in with Lachlan. He was busy assembling the herd ready to be led off with the stockmen. The herd would be followed by the riders on horseback who would be followed, in turn, by the pedestrian sponsors. They were almost ready.

Grace found the television crew and took them to meet the stockman and Marcus's cow beside the starting line. She would use the cow as a prop for the interview. She waited while a battery pack and microphone were clipped to her clothing and for the lighting and sound technicians to get into position. The muster wouldn't begin until after her interview but she was eager to get it over and done with.

The reporter gave a summary of the event before introducing her. 'I have Grace Gibson with me. She is the renal transplant co-ordinator at the Kirribilli General Hospital and one of the event organisers. Grace, can you tell me how much money you are hoping to raise and where it will be going?'

'Good morning, Grant. We are aiming to raise two hundred thousand dollars and we are already close to that target.' Fundraising had exceeded their expectations, thanks to Marcus's generous gift in Bill's name, and Grace was confident viewers would continue to donate online throughout the course of the muster.

'Money raised will be used to purchase dialysis machines for rural and remote hospitals and to train nursing staff to use them. Each machine costs thousands of dollars but, given that dialysis is required three times a week and takes several hours each time, you can imagine the disruptive impact it has on people's lives. Country people also have to factor in travel time to the hospital if dialysis can't be done locally, or have the expense, stress and upheaval of moving to the city.

'Supplying dialysis machines to country hospitals will save time and money and reduce stress, but a kidney transplant is even better than dialysis for the majority of people. It's a cheaper option but, even more important, the long-term outcomes are better. Thank you to everyone who has already donated, but if you haven't yet donated to this cause and would like to, our website is up on the screen and you will also find more information about organ donation, living or deceased, there too. And now let's get this mob on the bridge.'

Grace stepped back and unclipped her microphone, waiting as an assistant unhooked the power pack. She made her way to the back of the herd where she had planned to follow behind with the walkers. She watched as the cattle started moving sedately onto the access ramp ready to traverse the bridge. She couldn't help the grin that spread across her face. It was really happening.

The cattle passed by and the horses began to follow. The noise level increased slightly as riders chatted as they guided their horses onto the ramp. Grace stepped further to one side, making room as she listened to the snippets of conversations in passing.

'Grace?'

A horse stopped beside her right shoulder and she looked up as she heard her name. Marcus was looking down at her.

She blinked, not sure she could trust her eyes. Was she imagining him?

'Marcus?'

He smiled at her, his teeth white in contrast to the designer stubble that darkened his jaw. He wore a padded vest to combat the crisp morning air. Under the vest, with its familiar embroidered longhorn logo, he wore a checked shirt, along with jeans that moulded to his thighs and stockman's riding boots. He looked good on horseback. He looked good in general. Actually, he looked better than good.

'What are you doing here?'

'I told you I'd ride.'

Her heart was racing. 'But that was before you left.'

'I came back. Will you ride with me?'

The horse nuzzled Grace and she lifted her hand and rubbed its face and looked at it for the first time as she wondered where Marcus had got a horse from. It looked familiar and seemed to recognise her. She frowned. 'Is this one of Lachlan's horses?'

He nodded. 'It's Percival.'

'I don't understand.'

'Hop up here with me and I'll tell you everything.'

He leant over in the saddle and held out his hand. The horse was an Arab and could easily manage to carry them both the relatively short distance over the bridge. Grace reached out and put her hand in his. His fingers closed around hers, warm and safe. Her palm tingled and her heart beat increased its pace a little further. He lifted her off her feet in one smooth movement and swung her into position behind him. She tucked herself tightly against him and wrapped her arms around his waist. She rested her head on his back, feeling the warmth of his body seep into her bones. She could smell the tang of the ocean, the fresh saltiness in the air as Marcus's familiar scent mingled with the smell of the sea.

She closed her eyes and breathed him in.

She'd missed him. She gave herself a few moments to enjoy having him back in her arms, to enjoy the feel of him. This was where she belonged. With him. She knew it. She recognised it. She just wished he did too.

Marcus sat easily in the saddle. He held the reins loosely and threaded his fingers through Grace's as he guided Percival forward with slight pressure from his knees.

'I don't understand how you're here, and how you've got Percival too,' Grace said.

'I will explain it all once we cross the bridge but for now I want you to have a look around and take all this in. You and Merridy have done an amazing job to bring this to fruition and I want you to savour the moment. You should be really proud of what you've achieved here.'

His advice was good and Grace listened to it. He was here and his words suggested they would have time to talk later. While the muster would take a couple of hours, Grace knew it would seem to pass in the blink of an eye. She wouldn't get this opportunity again. She needed to embrace it.

The view from horseback was incredible.

Lines of cattle stretched in front of them and the walkers stretched out behind them. The walkway had become a functioning stock route once more. The sky was clear and bright as the sun began to warm the air. Helicopters circled the bridge and boats zipped across the harbour beneath them. It was a beautiful day. And Marcus was back. It was a perfect day.

By the time they reached the south side of the bridge the crowd was buzzing. On an adrenalin high from the experience, people milled around, reliving the muster and checking out the social media posts.

'Do you want to dismount and join in?' Marcus asked her.

Grace looked at the crowd. She had no desire to change her position. She was happy right where she was, with her arms wrapped around Marcus. Lachlan and Hamish would supervise loading the cattle and horses back onto the trucks that had followed them across the bridge and she suspected it was going to take longer than they'd anticipated as people did not seem eager to disperse. She had no urgent tasks to attend to. No one needed her right this minute. 'No,' she said with a shake of her head.

She didn't know what she'd expected Marcus to do next but she definitely hadn't expected him to keep on riding. 'Where are you going?' she asked as he turned the horse west and headed away from the bridge. 'We need to load Percival onto a truck.'

'Your family have everything under control, we've got some time. You're free to come with me, if you wish.'

She didn't need to think about her answer. 'I wish,' she said.

Marcus directed Percival up Observatory Hill, where he dismounted beside the old bandstand. He looped the horse's reins around the wooden balustrade and lifted Grace down before taking her hand and leading her up the steps into the rotunda, where they had a view back across the harbour past the bridge to Luna Park.

Grace wasn't interested in the view any more. Marcus was watching her intently and she couldn't think about anything other than the fact that he was back and looking at her like he never wanted to let her go.

He lifted his hand and ran his fingers over her cheek and Grace's breath caught in her throat. 'I missed you,' he said.

She wanted to reach up and hold his hand against her face. She wanted to keep him close for ever. 'I missed you too,' she replied, 'but I'm still confused as to what you're doing here.'

He wrapped his arms around her and held her close. 'I've been in Toowoomba. I flew over to see Lachlan and Merridy about the sale of Bill's—my—land. I told them I intended to come down to Sydney for the Herd across the Harbour and one thing led to another and Lachlan offered to lend me a horse. I wanted to see you, although I hadn't expected such a huge crowd. I was really worried I wouldn't find you.'

'I'm glad you did.'

'Are you?'

'I think so,' she said with some nervousness. Last time they'd had a face-to-face conversation it hadn't unfolded as she'd anticipated and she needed to know what had really brought him back. 'But I guess it depends on why you're here.'

'I'm here for you.' He lifted a strand of her hair and tucked it behind one ear. Grace's heart stuttered as his fingers brushed over her skin. 'I'm sorry I left you to go back to Perth. I should have asked you to come with me.'

'Why didn't you?'

'Because I wanted to save myself the pain of rejection. I've been trying to get away from my past and although you've shown me that my past can't hurt me any more, I was still afraid that no one could love me. That *you* couldn't love me. My parents both chose to prioritise other things over me. My mother ran away to start a different life with a new man, my father sought oblivion in the bottle. They didn't choose me.

'How could you love me if my own parents didn't? Your family is here, your work is here, your life is here. What could I offer you? I was afraid you wouldn't choose me and I was too scared to find out, but the pain of not having you, of knowing that I'd lost you and wondering if that was inevitable or if it was my own fault, was even worse. I thought you were better off without me. I didn't think I was enough for you. I didn't know if I could make you happy.'

Grace regretted the fact that she hadn't made her feelings clear to Marcus before he'd gone back to Perth. It was uncharacteristic of her to hold her tongue but she knew why she'd kept quiet. She'd been afraid of getting her heart broken, just as Lola had warned her. This was her second chance at happiness. He was here, he'd come back for her and she knew he needed to hear how she felt. 'You excite me, delight me, content me.' She smiled. 'And sometimes frustrate me, but all that is so much more than just making me happy. You make me feel alive. You let me breathe. I have been holding my breath for so long, waiting for something, but it wasn't something in the end, it was someone. It was you.'

'Me? You want me?'

'I want you.'

'Even with all my demons?'

'Demons?'

'Who knows what I've inherited from my parents? My mother's abandonment tendencies, my father's addictions? What if I break your heart?'

'Marcus.' Grace took his hands in hers, stilling him, making him listen. 'Look at everything you have achieved in the past twenty years. How far you've come. The choices you've made have been good ones. I don't think you have abandonment tendencies—you've stuck with your studies, you've come back for me, you've chosen wisely. You are a good man and you deserve good things in your life. You should have asked me if I wanted to be with you,' she told him. 'I would have chosen you.'

'Am I enough for you?'

'You are enough for me. You are *everything* for me.' He needed to know he had her love and commitment. He needed to know she wouldn't leave him, that he could trust her to stay. That he could trust her to give him her word and to keep it. 'Since the first moment I saw you again on the day of the press conference I was drawn to you. You captured my heart and you have it still.

'I need you to believe in me,' she said. 'I need you to believe in us. You have to believe me when I tell you that I will not leave you, that I will not choose someone or something else over you because if you are always waiting or expecting me to leave you, this won't work. I can't build a relationship without trust. Or love. I have always been open and honest with you. You just need to ask for my opinion or my thoughts and I will give them to you. Willingly. I will give you everything willingly. I will be here for you always. I love you and I choose you. Together we can be happy, so why don't you ask me again to come to Perth with you?'

'No.'

'No?' she asked, flinching.

'I've been offered a job back here. At Kirribilli General. Andrew Murray is retiring. So I thought, if you would have me back, I'll take the job and move to Sydney.'

She couldn't stop the smile that spread across her face. He was really coming back. To her. 'Are you sure this is what you want?'

His smile matched hers. 'I have never been more sure of anything in my life. You are everything I need. You have put me back together and you make me feel that nothing is impossible. Not even love. I'm in love with you, Grace—'

'You love me?' she gasped.

'I love you so much. I want a life with you, a family with you. I want to grow old with you but I am really here to ask you one thing.' He dropped to one knee and Grace's smile grew even wider. 'I came back to ask you if you would be my wife. I love you and I don't ever want to let you go. If you will have me, I promise to spend the rest of my life making you happy, making you proud and making you so crazy about me that you will wonder how you lived without me.'

'I'm already crazy about you.' She knelt down with him and cupped his face in her hands, pulling him towards her until their lips were millimetres apart. 'I love you too and, yes, I will marry you,' she said, seconds before he kissed her.

And with that kiss they sealed their future, their promises and their love.

* * * * *

LET'S TALK

Romance

For exclusive extracts, competitions and special offers, find us online:

- ■ facebook.com/millsandboon
- ◉ @millsandboonuk
- 🐦 @millsandboon

Or get in touch on 0844 844 1351*

For all the latest titles coming soon, visit millsandboon.co.uk/nextmonth

*Calls cost 7p per minute plus your phone company's price per minute access charge

Want even more
ROMANCE?

Join our bookclub today!

'Mills & Boon books, the perfect way to escape for an hour or so.'

Miss W. Dyer

'Excellent service, promptly delivered and very good subscription choices.'

Miss A. Pearson

'You get fantastic special offers and the chance to get books before they hit the shops'

Mrs V. Hall

Visit millsandbook.co.uk/Bookclub and save on brand new books.

MILLS & BOON